Other books by the author:

Starlight
Pit Bull
Overgrown with Love
The Angel of the Garden
A Song for Alice Loom
Eating Mississippi
The Dream of the Red Road
Pulpwood
Dream Fishing

Plumb's Bluff

Scott Ely

Livingston Press
The University of West Alabama

Plumb's Bluff

CHAPTER ONE

Chalmers Plumb casually paddled the canoe around the outside curve of the bend, the air charged with mist from the shoal at his back. As he floated under a canopy of river birch, their new green leaves not yet large enough to close out the blue sky, he turned the canoe out of the slack water and into the current and felt the power of the river against the paddle blade, the push traveling up his arm and into his shoulder. He sensed the subtle vectors of eddy and crosscurrent, the geography of a powerful river that could drown him or destroy his boat.

He was on the north Alabama River looking for the killers of his father. Randall Plumb had been caught like a piece of trash on a single strand of barbed wire strung in a rapid that bore his name. Drowned. No chance for him at all. All night Chalmers had kept the boat in an eddy, waiting for someone to string wire again at Plumb's Run. He'd never spent the whole night there. But this night as he'd sat in the boat in the moonlight and listened to the pulse of the water and breathed the wet air and smelled the green stink of the hillside trees, he'd let himself be so caught up in the rhythms of the river that the lightening of the sky over the ridge and the appearance of the morning star came as a surprise. As the sun rose over the ridge, he'd looked down for a moment at the reflection of his face in the eddy, obscured here and there by the turbulence, so it was just any human face, no reason at all for it to be his, and then took the boat out of the eddy and down through the rapid. He'd felt lightheaded and empty.

Since his father's death, he'd spent many a moonlit night on the river. Usually he left the rapid around midnight. He'd get only a few hours of sleep before returning to his job as a strip mine blaster.

The rapid was famous for its undercut rocks. To run it you had to make precise, quick moves. If you made a mistake, if your boat filled with water and you had to swim, the rocks were waiting. The powerful current would pin you against a rock and roll you under and you would die.

People had started calling the rapid Plumb's Run after his father began running it on moonlit nights, soon after his return from Vietnam. Now the name was in all the guidebooks. Until his father's death Chalmers had never run it alone in the moonlight and hadn't known anyone, no matter how skilled, who had. Most people did it in teams in the daytime, setting up rescue ropes at the difficult places.

In an ammo box lashed to a thwart was his father's .44. Now and then the canoe had taken on water, but the pistol, its bluing perfect, remained dry and unscratched in the cocoon of foam he'd carved out for it. He changed the angle of the paddle blade and brought the boat close to the moss and fern-covered bank where later in the season cardinal flowers would burst out red against the green. On the steep hillside wild hydrangeas were in bloom, their white blossoms scattered among the windfalls of brown leaves. The breeze tossed the branches of the oaks and hickories, exposing the pale green undersides of the leaves.

Ahead, the Nectar Bridge, pine planks laid over cypress timbers, came into view. He caught a glimpse of three figures standing on the planks and a white van. Then he ducked his head to avoid the overhanging branches of a clump of serviceberries and was left unsure whether the figures were men or women.

Since it was Sunday, Brother Sprott was probably baptizing those who'd come to Jesus in the river. Chalmers had been baptized at the bridge. That day his family had stood on the planks and watched.

He looked at the bridge again. The figures hadn't moved. He didn't see a baptism group gathered by the water. Now one of the figures was moving, but the other two were still. They were all looking out over the big pool, not at the baptismal shallows. The two motionless ones were small, the size of children. One was wearing a strange sort of coat whose surface appeared to be covered with feathers. Chalmers was reminded of the wind ruffling the feathers of vultures at roost in a dead tree. The people must be watching something, maybe a snake swimming across the deep pool.

Then the center figure, now he saw it was a woman, dropped off the bridge. Something was tied around her neck. Chalmers hesitated only for a moment as he waited for the two small figures to react. They didn't. He put his head down, digging the paddle into the water. He took the short powerful strokes of a racer, and the canoe shot across the water.

In that moment, just as he reached the deep pool and was looking for her beneath the water, trying to see through the glare, but before he went in after her, he realized that the figures on the bridge were statues: one had the head of a man attached to the body of a bird, the feathers still rippling in the breeze; the other had the head of a woman and the body of an insect, her black thorax glistening in the sunlight.

Chalmers went over the side into the pool, the greenish water, colored by some mineral, perfectly clear. The cold water made his head hurt. He saw the woman, her long hair streaming out in the current. Either end of the rope was tied to a small block of dark marble, lighter colored veins snaking through the stone. The marble had been carved on one side in a jagged pattern like the teeth of an alligator. He swam down to her. The pool was no more than ten or twelve feet deep.

As he lifted the rope, which luckily she'd draped carelessly over her neck like a scarf instead of tying it, she looked at him. She was holding her breath; her eyes were dark, like two bits of coal. She shook her head and groped for the rope, her body light in the water, stirring up clouds of sediment with her hands. He put his hand on her shoulder. She pushed it away. Other pieces of marble were in the pool, grotesque figures that resembled nothing he'd ever seen. They were all straight lines and hard edges and had come to rest at crazy angles.

Chalmers' lungs were beginning to burn. The woman looked at him, her face strangely calm, and released a few bubbles of air. She wasn't breathing water yet; she hadn't made up her mind about dying. He came at her from behind and got his arm around her neck while she was searching for the rope. Then he pulled her to the surface.

She screamed something in a strange language, the sound echoing off the clay banks. As she slipped under the water again, he caught her arm. She clawed at his face. He dived, taking hold of her legs and spinning her around. Then from behind he got a grip on her hair and towed her to shore. They both lay panting on a gravel bar whose water-washed stones felt smooth and warm against his palms and smelled faintly of fish.

She was a pretty woman, not much older than Chalmers, who was two years out of high school. She had an oval face and a nose with hard clean lines, like a piece of fractured rock.

The woman spoke something again, the words liquid but alien, like a bird song he'd never heard before.

Chalmers looked up at the bridge where the two statues stared off down the river. Too bad Brother Sprott wasn't bringing a baptism party down the gravel road. Those new converts would think he was leading them into Hell.

Lately Chalmers had given up on church. He'd done it because Brother Sprott had refused his father burial in the graveyard behind the church, even though Randall Plumb had been baptized in the Nectar Pool by Mason Sprott's predecessor. Brother Sprott had said that counted as nothing, that Randall Plumb hadn't set foot inside the church since he went off to fight in Vietnam.

Quitting church hadn't been an easy thing for Chalmers. Now he felt disconnected. His relatives still spoke to him, all those cousins, but he had removed himself from the web of kinship whose center was the Nectar Bridge Church. In a way he'd become invisible. No one wanted to acknowledge he was going to Hell. Most believed his father had already found the path for him to follow. Sometimes he felt as if he were entering the most difficult part of Plumb's Run and had had the paddle snap in his hands, the current sweeping him toward one of those undercut rocks.

She was breathing hard, her breath coming in ragged gasps. Gradually she became calmer.

"Leave me in tranquility," she said.

Her English was thickly accented, but he had no trouble understanding.

"You about drowned us both," he said.

"I wish to die," she said.

"Then all you had to do was take a big breath of water while you were down there. Why do you want to die?"

She didn't reply.

She had the frightened look of an animal at bay. A streak of gray mud was smeared across her left cheek; her black eyes darted back and forth. She fixed them on the water.

"Why?" he asked again.

"I cannot forget."

"Forget what?"

She appeared to be thinking hard as if she were having trouble recalling exactly what it was that caused her to jump off the bridge. Her accent sounded eastern European. He recalled striking Polish steelworkers he'd seen on TV. Perhaps she hadn't really understood his questions.

"Who are you?"

"Livia. I—" She hesitated. "Pardon me, my English leaves me."

Now her breath came again in ragged gasps.

Her lip was bleeding. He wondered if she'd bit it or if he'd hit her with an elbow as they struggled in the water.

"What were you doing down there?" he asked.

"Dying," she said.

"I'm against dying. I'm against forgetting too."

She smiled at him.

They sat together on the gravel. She was silent for a time. He listened to the gurgle of the river past the bridge footers and to the songs of the birds. Her breathing became steady and regular.

Then Livia told him she was from Romania. She was an artist, a sculptor. Married to an American painter from Mobile. Livia had gone to sleep with him one night only a few days ago and woke in the morning to find him dead. It all came out of her in a rush, spoken in an English occasionally mixed with Romanian words.

"His dying was my great surprise," she said.

Chalmers imagined her waking in the night and reaching out to feel her dead husband's body lying still and cold beside her. It must have been terrible. That must be what she wanted to forget.

"That doesn't mean you should kill yourself," Chalmers said.

Chalmers considered telling her about his father but decided against it. For the first time he noticed the red mark the rope had left on her neck.

He pictured the strange pieces of sculpture at the bottom of the pool and wondered why she wanted to look at them as she drowned.

"Why'd you toss that marble in the river?"

He stood up and tried to look into the pool. The sun was in his eyes. He thought he saw a gar, but there was no sign of the statues he knew were there.

"Yes," she said. "I do it."

He was glad she hadn't thrown the creatures on the bridge into the river. He'd have hated to dive down into that greenish water and run into them.

She stood up and started to wade into the river.

"Wait," he said.

He grabbed her arm.

"My sculptures," she said.

Then he released her. She paused and peeled off her wet clothes, keeping her back to him. He glanced briefly at the strong curve of her back and at her buttocks and legs. She was beautiful. He felt a pleasant floating feeling, and then a quietness, just like at that moment when he set the charges off and the explosion sent a ripple through the cut where he'd planted the explosive, and smoke and dust rose into the air, but before there was sound. He felt uncomfortable staring, afraid she was going to turn and catch him.

She swam across the pool with smooth, powerful strokes. He retrieved the canoe where it had come to rest against the bank. Then he paddled out into the pool. She dived. He counted slowly to thirty as he stared into the pool, the sun at his back, watching her struggle with a piece of sculpture. It was as if she were performing some slow underwater dance.

Then she pushed off from the bottom, puffs of sediment exploding from beneath her feet, and rose to the surface. She smiled at him, her black hair plastered against her head. She cradled the piece against her breasts; she was breathing hard. The weight of it kept pulling her under as she treaded water. She kicked herself to the surface, emerging laughing.

He liked to hear her laugh. He'd never known anyone who'd tried to commit suicide. It was hard for him to imagine someone laughing one moment and jumping off a bridge the next. So maybe for the time being she was safe from that.

"Here," she said. "Here."

He sculled the canoe over to her and took the piece into the boat. The square block of marble was heavier than he'd imagined. A side was dark with mud; a slot filled with teeth was cut into one face. He lay the piece carefully in the bottom of the canoe, the mud-smeared side gritty against the smooth plastic. She dived again.

She made six dives, her dark body disappearing into the clear green water.

"Done," she said, as she emerged with the last piece.

She was breathing hard.

The pieces lay about on the bottom of the canoe, their weight making the boat handle sluggishly. It was as if he'd been checking turtle traps and had filled the canoe with cooters. She swam across the pool and stood on the gravel, wringing out her clothes. He looked at her, the sun on her breasts, a bar of light falling across her thighs just below the patch of hair. She waved at him and smiled.

He began carrying the pieces up to her van, thinking of her carving those dangerous looking teeth. The two figures stared upstream, the bird man's feathers ruffled by the breeze and the sun shining brilliantly off the insect woman's body.

CHAPTER TWO

They put his canoe on top of the van and his mountain bike inside. He'd left the bike at the bridge earlier to run the shuttle to his truck that he'd left at Plumb's Bluff, the place he launched the canoe. As Chalmers drove, Livia sat in the front seat of the van, feeling as if she were half asleep or dreaming. They'd left the bridge and climbed a hill. Instead of tall vine-covered trees, the hillsides were now covered with a scrubby oak growing out of red earth. She knew such trees in Romania. The river had been like a tunnel though that thick greenness: mosses, cane, masses of flower bushes with pink and white flowers, white-blossomed dogwoods, vines, patches of briar. Some of the vines, grapevines Michael had called them, were as thick as one of her legs. Now the land had a feeling of aridness, even sterility that made her uncomfortable.

She felt herself trembling. She had been at the bottom of the pool, determined to die, and then this boy had appeared. At first she thought he was part of death. In her childhood she'd heard tales of spirits that inhabited deep pools in rivers and lakes. During the day they slept, but at night they'd awaken and lie in wait for people so foolish as to wander the mountains in the darkness. This boy had come swimming down to her, his long blond hair trailing out behind him. And she'd thought momentarily, before she realized what he was, that she was going to have a beautiful death.

Now the boy wasn't looking at her but concentrating on the road. Then he glanced at her and smiled. She smiled back.

They traveled on the gravel road until it intersected with a narrow blacktop one. This road went up and down over the hills. Every now and then they passed a place where the land was denuded, only a few patches of scraggly pines growing on the eroded soil. Here the land was truly barren, a vacantness that the pines had no hope of ever filling.

"Strip mine," the boy said.

And she wondered exactly what that meant but decided not to ask questions. She was still deep inside herself, lost in that dream of death: the bridge, the green water, the unfamiliar trees, a bird that flew over the pool with white-banded wings giving a sharp cry.

Then they passed a place where half of a hillside had been ripped away. She could see machines, including a big crane with a bucket attached. A line of dump trucks was parked next to it. All the machinery was motionless. She remembered it was Sunday.

The boy noticed she was looking at the machines.

"Dragline," he said.

She again remembered the bottom of the pool, the remembering like the shock of the cold water on her body. She'd opened her eyes and looked at her sculptures lying about on the bottom. A fish with a long thin nose, which reminded her of a European pike, swam by. As it made a pass at a school of minnows, it opened its mouth, revealing rows of needle-like teeth.

How like my sculptures, she'd thought.

"I work there," he said.

They were well past the mine, and she looked back at it. She imagined him driving one of the trucks.

The road ran into a highway. A green sign said it was forty-five miles to Birmingham and eight miles to Susan Moore. They went in the direction of Susan Moore. She wondered where they were going but decided she didn't care. They crossed a bridge over a river. Below was a rapids, the surface of the river dotted with white water. The sound of the rapids, a steady rush, came up to her over the hiss of the tires on the concrete. The hillsides were covered with trees, all the leaves a pale shade of green. Here and there were dark clumps of pines.

Now she was truly free of the dream of death, of the anticipation of floating about among her sculptures. They passed a billboard advertising gasoline and one with the picture of a chain saw on it. Then they went past a grove of peach trees as they climbed the hill above the bridge. An empty wooden shack, made of unpainted plywood and open on one side, bore a sign that read FRESH PEACHES. She had seen the same scenery of billboards and tree-covered hills and little towns ever since she first came to visit these hills above Birmingham.

He slowed the van and made a left turn. At the intersection of the gravel road with the highway there was a church. It was like all the others she had seen in the hills, small and painted white. She had never imagined that people would find the need of so many churches. There was a portable sign on the lawn in front of the church: PANCAKE SUPPER, APRIL 28. Black letters against a white background.

They left the church behind and went along the road past a pasture dotted with cows. Someone was plowing a field with a tractor. She watched him turn and stare at the van. The boy waved to him and the man waved back. Then the road lost elevation some and went into a stand of pines. There were pine needles on the road. The tires made a smooth, soft sound against them.

Ahead was something white and shiny, which in a moment she realized was a trailer. The van came into a clearing. A metal building was next to it. A rack held several canoes. One was red, another green, but the rest were a rich golden color. She was reminded of fields of ripe wheat. They were on the edge of a bluff, for she could see the empty space above what she guessed was the river.

"Plumb's Bluff," the boy said.

He smiled at her.

"Plumb's Bluff," she said.

He laughed.

"That's right," he said. "You got it exactly right."

Livia felt easy with this boy whose clothes and hair were still wet from the river. She remembered the look in his eyes when he saw her at the bottom of the pool, a look of amazement, almost reverence. That was it, she thought, thinking as always in Romanian. Reverence.

"Let's get out of these wet clothes," he said. "And get something to eat. I'm hungry."

His voice was soft and slow. She liked that.

He went into the trailer. She changed too, taking clothes from a suitcase in the back of the van.

They sat at a picnic table overlooking the river under the shade of big poplars and pines. Chalmers had helped his father make the table one Sunday afternoon when Chalmers was twelve, the date carved on one of the benches. Below was a rapid where he'd set his practice gates. In the stand of big pines were the canoe shop and the trailer where he lived.

They were eating Brunswick stew. She ate quickly, her head lowered over the bowl.

"This meat?" she asked.

"Squirrel," he said.

Livia wasn't quite sure what he'd said, so she asked again.

"Squirrel," he said.

This time he spoke the word slowly and carefully.

She knew what they were but hadn't imagined that people ate them. She looked down at her bowl.

"It's good meat," he said.

She smiled at him and took a bite to show that she appreciated what he'd given her.

It was squirrel Chalmers had shot. There was always squirrel or rabbit or deer in the freezer. Chalmers also kept a garden. He'd grown the corn and beans and peppers that were in the stew. There were jars of vegetables stored in a room at the rear of the shop.

Livia wiped out her bowl with a piece of bread.

"More?" he asked.

She shook her head.

"Good," she said.

She smiled at him, but as she did so she began to cry. A tear rolled down her cheek. She didn't wipe it off. She wanted to be back in that dream. She'd looked up and seen the sky through the leaves. Then he'd come, the impact of his body shattering her field of vision and destroying her dream of death.

"We'll have us a drink," he said.

She looked up at him but said nothing. Chalmers was unsure whether he should leave her sitting so close to the edge of the bluff.

"Whiskey?" she asked.

"Yes," he said.

"Good."

"I've got beer."

"No, whiskey is good. Slivovic would be better. But whiskey

is good."

She thought of how good the slivovic would taste, burning her throat and mouth, making her feel warm inside. Chalmers had no idea what slivovic was.

He went to the trailer and returned with the bottle. She was sitting on top of the table now, her feet on one of the benches.

They drank the whiskey warm out of coffee cups. Livia found it smoother than slivovic. She told him she'd come to the hills to work. She planned to use local marble.

"No marble up here," he said. "They've got that over in Georgia."

Michael had told her about the marble in the hills, how there were huge quarries. It was a beautiful white marble.

"It is here," she said.

She knew that she'd surely left that dream of death because she was talking about work now. New work. But despite what he said about the marble, she believed it was there. Just as Michael had said.

"Well, you look all you want."

"I come here for marble."

She hoped he was understanding what she was saying.

Chalmers listened carefully to the woman. She'd spoken the words slowly. It was clear she believed there was marble in the hills. He wasn't going to insist there wasn't any. He didn't want to upset her.

"Well, maybe," he said. "I never heard of any coming out of a mine around here."

"Michael said it was here," she said. "You will find me marble?"

She looked at the boy. She imagined him working at one of the strip mines, his blond hair a bright spot against the coal.

He'd told her he was a blaster. She imagined a series of huge explosions and chunks of coal sailing through the air.

"You'll be the first to know if I do," he said.

Chalmers felt good in the presence of the woman. She was different from the girls he took to movies in Birmingham. He supposed it was because she was foreign and older. It was hard to tell. She might be as old as twenty-five. Since his father's burial, he'd seen few people other than his cousin Edward. Because Brother Sprott had refused to let his father be buried in the graveyard at the church, Chalmers had done the job himself, his father lying in the grove of pines in the old family plot behind the trailer. They had stopped burying there a long time ago.

Grandmother Rosa came to her son's burial. It was one of the few times she'd ever been out to Plumb's Bluff. His grandmother and his father had avoided each other for as long as he could remember. When his father had come home from Vietnam and had gone to work for Rudy Blount, her rival, mother and son had drifted apart. Grandmother Rosa wanted the coal that lay beneath the thousand acres of land his father owned and that now belonged to Chalmers.

Chalmers' mother had died when he was a baby. She was buried in the Nectar Bridge graveyard. He and his grandmother had never been close. She'd tried to take the place of his mother, but he had, for some reason he couldn't explain, refused to let her.

She had come alone, no other kin. They were afraid of Brother Sprott. As he and Edward filled up the grave, he looked at her from time to time to see if she was crying. She might have been. But it was a cold, raw day, the pines soughing as the gusts ripped through them. And it could have just been that cold wind making her eyes water. Grandmother Rosa was tough. If she cried, she'd do it in private.

Chalmers had spoken his own words over his father, speaking of Randall Plumb's love of the land, a thousand acres of oaks and pines, and the river. Then he and Edward picked up the shovels. When Chalmers dropped the first shovelful of dirt on top of the plywood coffin he'd made with his own hands, the pebbles in the sandy soil rattling off it, Chalmers felt as if he'd stepped into a pool of quicksand in some swamp, sinking in the cold, wet grip of it into darkness. He'd stopped for a moment. Edward was working steadily. Then Chalmers put his head down and let himself be caught up in the rhythm of Edward's work.

"You think this is right?" his grandmother had asked.

They all stood together on the edge of the filled grave.

"I guess it is," Chalmers said.

"Without a Christian burial," she said.

Chalmers was cold. She didn't look cold. The wind tugged at her coat; the wind tossed her gray hair about.

"He's dead," Chalmers said. "Least he'll have the company of some Plumbs."

Edward was blowing on his hands.

"And his soul?" she asked. "Have you thought about that."

"I don't know about that," he said. "What I do know is his soul doesn't need the care of any preacher."

"I'd rather he be at the church," she said.

"He'll rest easy right here," he said.

"He might prefer to lie beside Alice," she said.

"Do you think God caused that boat trailer to come unhitched?" he'd heard his father once say to Grandmother Rosa. "Ask Brother Sprott about *that* being HIS plan."

To put an end to the discussion Chalmers took up Thoreau's *A Week on the Concord and Merrimack Rivers*. He read a few of his father's favorite passages from *Walden*. He ended with the one about Thoreau lying on the ice looking down at a snake resting on the bottom of the pond. His father had liked to do that on the river, drift in the canoe in a still pool and search for snakes lying on the bottom, particularly the big ones banded in bright colors: red and yellow against the green water. It was hard to read in the wind, which tugged at the pages of the book and made his words seem small as it hummed in the tops of the pines, carrying the sound of his voice away toward the river.

Chalmers had never been as interested in Thoreau as his father was. A Red Cross girl had given his father the copy of *Walden* when his father arrived in Vietnam. Chalmers liked Edward Abbey better or Peter Matthiessen or lately Annie Dillard. Although Chalmers had never done particularly well in school, he liked to read books about rivers and nature. His father hated TV so they never had a set. After they came home from the mine and had eaten, they'd sit in the living room of the trailer and read together. Sometimes his father read Thoreau aloud to him.

After he finished the passages, he expected that his grandmother would produce a Bible and read a few verses. But she did nothing. He stood there with the book in his hand, the wind buffeting all of them, and waited for her to speak.

"I'd rather he was lying at the church," she said.

Those were the last words she spoke.

He stood alone over the grave while Edward walked her to the car. She'd taken Edward's arm, but she walked very erect and straight. Not like an old woman at all. He'd never seen her lean against a chair back at dinner. He imagined it was hard walking across the carpet of pine needles in a pair of heels.

Chalmers now looked at the woman. Her hair had dried. It was very fine, not coarse like he'd expected, dropping in a mane about her shoulders. Again he felt that floating sensation that was now like falling, as if he'd taken his boat over a drop which turned out to have no bottom. He tried to imagine how her hair would feel against his hands.

"You can stay here," he said.

She explained that she and her husband had taken a cabin for several months at an artists' retreat on Bankhead Lake. He told her again he was sorry he was dead. She seemed to take no notice of his words.

"I cannot sleep in that cabin," she said.

"I can imagine," he said.

"Now I will work."

"That's good. But you shouldn't be alone."

She smiled at him and brushed a strand of hair out of her eyes.

"You can work here," he said.

Livia thought of the boy's appearance as some sort of sign. She'd learned to trust such fortuitous happenings. She'd survived the death of her family by chance; she escaped from Romania by chance. And she'd met Michael in France in the same way. She'd sat down at a table in a Paris cafe, turned her head, and there he was. Now that Michael was dead she preferred to let herself drift. The boy had kept her from dying so she would stay here for a time. Then she'd go find those cliffs of white marble Michael had told her about.

Her cup was empty, and he poured her another drink. It was getting late in the afternoon, the sun low over the trees behind them. Kayaks were coming down through the rapid. This time of year the whitewater sections of the river were often crowded.

"I stay this night," she said.

"As long as you want," he said.

"A beautiful river?"

"Yes."

They both looked down at the river. The kayaks were gone. It was dark over the rapid now; he could no longer see the wires on which hung the striped gate poles. The gates were arranged in pairs: a red-striped upstream gate and a green-striped downstream gate. A racer went through a downstream gate and then had to turn the canoe into an eddy and paddle through the upstream gate. The first time Chalmers had seen his father bring a canoe to a dead stop in a swift current, spin it with a paddle stroke, and shoot it through the upstream gate, he'd thought he was watching magic.

Chalmers had been dreaming of the river at night. The water became mixed with his blood so that it flowed in his veins. Gar fed in the shoals and spotted bass floated at the bottom of the deep clear pools and otters played tag among midstream rocks. White spider lilies bobbed in the current. And sometimes the flow bore him past lilies and fish and otters, gently sweeping him toward his father, who lay reclined at the bottom of the river, his hair filled with weeds. But he was smiling, a soft smile of life, not the grin of death.

She lit a cigarette, taking a match out of the pocket of her jeans and striking it against the tabletop. Since his father's death, no woman had sat on that table. The girls from his high school class were no longer interested in him. Some were married; others had gone to work in Birmingham or Atlanta. But that was all right. He'd train and work at the mine and wait for his chance to catch someone stringing wire. Right now that was enough.

"Why do you take a pistol on the river?" she asked.

She'd watched him remove it from the ammo box. Now she looked up into the treetops, waiting for him to answer.

"Snakes," he said.

She paused a moment.

"Chalmers, I am thankful you come for me," she said.

She took a long drag on the cigarette. Her lip was a little swollen. There was a cut on her right foot that needed to be cleaned.

"We'll find you some marble," he said. "You can work."

The inside of the van was filled with tools. He was thinking he could rig up a plastic tarp for her. She couldn't work inside the shop because of the dust. The shop had to be kept very clean. Dust in the fiberglass mixture could ruin the layup of a boat. And that pneumatic chisel of hers, those electric grinders, would stir up plenty of dust. At the end of a day at the mine he was covered with a thin layer of rock and coal dust. He'd never even think of going into the shop until he'd showered and changed clothes. He'd have to explain to her that she couldn't come into the shop with a cigarette. There were too many flammable and explosive solvents

Scott Ely

about.

"You said there is no marble," she said.

"None I've ever seen," he said.

"I have pieces I can work."

"Good."

"You like my work?"

"Yes."

Chalmers thought of the inhuman figures in the van. He wondered why she'd brought them with her. It was as if she were composing a picture when she jumped off the bridge. That made sense to him. She'd planned to turn her death into a final elaborate picture, surrounded by her sculptures, all teeth and hard edges.

"They are mean beautiful," he said.

Her face blossomed into a smile

"Yes, a terrible beauty," she said. "That is true."

He told her he'd make her a place to work.

"I work here a few days," she said.

She gestured with the cigarette as she talked, the tip describing arcs in the twilight. He realized he never wanted her to leave. But he'd have to wait to say something like that to her.

"You have always lived here?" she asked.

"Yes," he said.

His father had come home after Vietnam and put the trailer at Plumb's Bluff, the cancer perhaps already blossoming in his body from Agent Orange. He'd gone to Vietnam as a blaster. The Agent Orange detail had been punishment for refusing to demolish a Vietnamese village.

"Blow those hooches," the captain had said.

"No, sir, I can't," his father had said. "All these people own is in 'em. Tools and rice. They'll starve."

"Gooks."

"People, sir."

"You won't?"

"No, sir. Can't."

Chalmers had heard his father tell that story only once. His father had been a little drunk.

"I surprised myself," his father had said. "Until that day I hadn't thought that much about the killing. I was thinking about keeping me alive. Then there was that damn captain in my face."

Chalmers wondered how it must have felt to suddenly have it

all come crashing down on him.

Randall Plumb had built the shop on the land his father had willed him. The land Chalmers' grandmother now wanted. Once their ancestors had a house at the bluff. All that was left was a bit of the foundation and the family burial plot surrounded by a chain link fence.

Grandmother Rosa came by and asked him to sell every Easter Sunday after church. Under the land lay Pocahontas grade coal. Lately the price was up. His father had found refusing his mother uncomfortable, although he made jokes about it.

"I killed enough trees in Vietnam," his father had said.

If Chalmers' father had worked for her, become part of her mining company, then resisting would have been difficult.

Chalmers' father had promised Grandfather Plumb, when the old man lay on his deathbed, not to mine the thousand acres bordering the river. And Chalmers' father had made Chalmers promise, on more than one occasion, that he'd never sell the land.

So his father worked as a blaster at the mine, the one useful thing the Army had taught him and had, after Chalmers' mother's death, stopped attending the Nectar Bridge church.

Brother Sprott had come out to talk with him about his not going to church. He hadn't stayed long, and his father had never been willing to say what passed between them. Chalmers had kept going to church and had been baptized in the river by Brother Sprott. Now that he no longer went to church, he wondered if Brother Sprott was going to pay him a visit and what he would say when the preacher did.

Livia was sitting with her arms around her knees, her head laid sideways on them. She smiled at him. It was growing dark, but it was too early in the season for fireflies yet. In the late spring the open darkness over the rapid would be filled with them. He'd wait expectantly for that time in the early summer when their blinks became synchronized, an insect three feet above the river blinking at the same time one did high up in the pines, the gorge filled with one regular flash of cold light.

When they did that, it made his father uneasy.

"Thousands of parachute flares," his father liked to say.

"Love," Chalmers had said.

"Fireflies got no minds," his father said. "Blinking themselves to death."

Livia put her hand on his shoulder.

"Your mother?" she asked.

"Dead, when I was a baby," he said.

She had died in a car wreck. A man's boat trailer had come unhitched and sailed right through her windshield.

"Your father," Livia asked.

"Dead too," he said.

Later he would tell her what had happened and of the grave in the grove of pines.

"We are the same," Livia said.

She thought of her dead family and her dead husband.

"Yes," he said. "I think we are."

Livia was just an outline now on the table beside him.

"I'll sleep in the shop," he said. "You can have the trailer."

She put her hand on his arm.

"No, I make a bed in the van," she said.

He thought of her sleeping in the van with the statues. He hadn't seen a cot or even an air mattress. He wondered if she intended to stretch out on the front seat. But he was reluctant to ask such questions.

Chalmers went off to bed. He lay naked under the blanket, listening to the sound of the insects and the call of the night birds. The sounds were muted and seemed far away. The whiskey had all gone to his head and made his arms and legs feel heavy. As he waited for his head to clear and sleep to come, he imagined holding Livia in his arms.

CHAPTER THREE

Chalmers woke before sunrise. He ate breakfast, oatmeal and blueberries, and did his stretches. Then he took the training canoe, its hull a layup of fiberglass and Kevlar, off the rack. He moved carefully as he walked past the van, because he expected Livia was still asleep.

He carried the canoe over one shoulder and the wooden paddle in his free hand. Both the boat and the paddle were heavier than the ones he used in a race, the boat weighing in at thirty-five pounds instead of the race boat weight of twenty-five. He liked the graceful curve of the golden translucent layup, and the smell and feel of the cedar gunwale against his cheek. The boats were strong for their weight but fragile. A paddler couldn't run into a rock, as you could do in a plastic boat, and expect the canoe to survive.

There was a richness to the curves of the boats, a kind of feminine perfection and balance. Unexpectedly the image of Livia was before him, standing naked in the river, the light falling on her breasts.

He walked past the picnic table down the bluff path to the river. Every morning before he went to work he paddled the gates.

At the bottom he put the boat down on the bank. His right hamstring had felt tight all the way down the trail. As he sat on the thick carpet of rhododendron leaves and stretched out the muscle, he thought again of the death of his father. He supposed every time he put a boat in the water, he'd think of him.

His cousins had been at the trailer the night his father didn't come home. They all waited for him at the Nectar Bridge, but he never appeared.

"We'll go look at Plumb's Run," Chalmers had said.

"You planning on taking canoes?" Buck asked.

"Only way I know," Chalmers said.

"We could call the rescue squad," Edward said. "Maybe they could get a chopper from Birmingham."

"Chopper can't fly in the gorge at night," he said.

"And we can't get on that rapid at night," Buck said. "It's crazy."

"I'll lead," Chalmers said. "I'll set lines."

"You ain't run it at night," Buck said.

"Then don't go," Chalmers said. "I'll go alone."

Edward and Buck had looked at each other.

"We'll find your daddy sitting on a rock," Edward said.

They all laughed.

Chalmers hoped that was where they'd find him. His father could roll an open canoe if it flipped. He'd seen him paddle one upright plenty of times. They might well find him sitting on a rock, smoking one of the cigars he kept in a waterproof pouch.

Chalmers had been part of that web of kin then. That was why they'd gone with him. If the same thing happened tomorrow, they might wait on the chopper or let him go alone. Except Edward. He imagined Edward would go with him.

They had taken tandem canoes. No one said a word about the fact that they were thinking about the extra space needed to carry a dead or injured person. Buck and Edward were in one boat. Chalmers paddled alone. Above the rapid, the river narrowed down to fifty feet and ran fast with a cliff on one side and big timber on the other. The water was black under the moonlight, the moon slipping in and out of the branches of the new-leaved trees. On the timbered hillside moonlight fell on the white blossoms of the wild hydrangeas and muted the delicate petals and made them appear to hang heavy on their thin stems. A night bird called.

They all sat in an eddy at the head of Plumb's Run, their backs to the rapid, the bows of the canoes pointed upstream. Both canoes were equipped with pedestal seats and thigh straps. The empty space in the bow and sterns of the boats was filled with plastic air bags, lashed in place with mountain climbing rope. They'd slipped spare paddles under the rope. The bags helped keep out water if a gunwale slipped under, but their real purpose was to make the canoes ride high in the water if they flipped. Then a paddler might have a chance at righting a boat. A canoe filled with water weighed as much as a small car.

Chalmers tried to appear confident, but he was afraid of the rapid. Three times he'd made mistakes at tricky places and had been saved from injury or death only because someone threw him a rope.

"Somebody should walk down and set a rope," Buck said.

"We don't have time," Chalmers said. "Daddy could be pinned against a rock."

"Be careful," Edward said.

They all put on their helmets and tightened their thigh straps.

Chalmers felt his fear leave him, replaced by concern for his father.

He paddled out of the eddy and set up his boat for the first drop. It was one of four feet. The most immediate hazard was a rock in the center of the chute over the drop. It wasn't undercut, but a paddler had to make the drop upright and then immediately execute a ferry off to the left. After that was a hole and some big standing waves.

He went over the drop and came down on a paddle brace on his off side, the paddle acting like an outrigger. He didn't change hands. There wasn't time. He had to twist his body to make the maneuver. Then he spun the boat so the bow was upstream, the rock to his back, and ferried across behind the hole on the face of a big standing wave toward an eddy on the left side of the river. The canoe jerked and bucked in his hands as he paddled through some more standing waves. He had to be careful not to swamp, because only a few yards downstream undercut rocks waited. If he swamped, he'd surely lose the boat, and if he were unlucky, his life.

He completed the ferry smoothly and punched through the eddy line, spinning the boat in the eddy so the bow pointed upstream. He got out of the boat and climbed onto one of the rocks. He took a rescue rope out of a bag and waited for Buck and Edward. They came over the drop smoothly. Soon they were sitting in the eddy beside his canoe.

"It's going to be easy," Chalmers said.

"Sure," Edward said.

Buck didn't say anything.

They slipped from eddy to eddy and then ferried across the main current, the paddlers leaning hard downstream and the boats shooting across to lose only a few feet of downriver passage. The rapid was in the shape of an S. Soon they'd reached the middle of the S but had seen no sign of his father, no canoe pinned against a rock at one of the places where that might be likely to happen.

Buck and Edward came to rest behind a boulder next to the shore, their boat rocking as it was pulled back and forth by the turbulence inside the eddy. Buck was bailing out water with a plastic milk carton whose bottom had been cut off. Chalmers stood with the rescue rope in his hands. The rush of the water was in their ears.

"We almost lost it," Buck said.

Edward laughed.

"Only took on a little water," Edward said. "We should do this every night." Edward looked downriver, the water spotted with patches of white. Here the current was particularly powerful. "Your daddy's probably at the trailer. Drinking whiskey and wondering where you are."

"Maybe," Chalmers said.

Chalmers walked along the bare rock, followed by his cousins. He played his light into the river to scout the difficult section. Something glinted in the light, and he followed the single strand of barbed wire tied to a big poplar, its limbs overhanging the rapid. The river was eating away at its roots and one day would topple it.

Then the others' lights were on it. Caught in the wire was a body. The blue life vest and the red helmet came into view as the body bobbed up and down, swinging in the water on the arc formed by the wire. He knew PLUMB was written across the back of the jacket in large block letters.

"Father!" Chalmers cried.

Chalmers knelt on the rock and hit it hard with his closed fist, feeling the skin of his knuckles slough away against the lichen-covered granite. The hard edges of the pain felt good; it made river and rock and the star-filled sky clear and brilliant in his mind. He looked at his father's body again, something in him hoping it was not going to be there, that this was just a log or a lard tub caught up in the wire. He forced himself to look at it, thinking of the touch of his father's hands on his as Randall Plumb taught him that first time how to pull a draw-knife along the piece of heart-of-pine that was to become a canoe paddle.

The others played their lights on the body. Chalmers squatted and put his hand on the wire. The cold water rushed against his hand. The wire was singing, vibrating, as the water pushed against the weight of the body and pulled the wire taut.

No way for his father to see the wire. It had been strung by someone who knew his father's fondness for moonlight runs on the river, who knew that he never scouted any of Plumb's Run, no matter what the water level. His father was famous for that, running it blind.

Then his cousins were putting their hands on him, stroking him as if he were a nervous horse.

"We'll cut it," Buck said.

Edward agreed.

"No," Chalmers said. "The river'll get him."

He imagined his father swept downstream, rolled up in the wire that would have a life of its own in the current, and maybe the wire would become snagged on an underwater tree trunk. It could take days to find him. He would be eaten by turtles.

"We'll put a rope on the wire and cut it," Buck said.

Chalmers shook his head. He wanted to lay his hands on his father; he wanted to pull him off the barbs.

"I reckon you can do what you want," Edward said.

So Buck ferried a rope across, a carabineer tied to the center, and secured it to a tree. Then with Edward in the bow and Chalmers in the stern, they set the canoe parallel to the current. Edward worked his way along the rope. He reached the carabineer and slipped a rope into it. Buck adjusted the rope until the canoe was positioned directly above the body. Edward lowered the canoe toward Chalmers' father.

Chalmers reached out, cautiously as a cat, and put his hand on his father, wincing at the coldness of the body. Fish he'd pulled out of the river felt like this. The canoe bounced in the current.

The body was heavy, as if it were a sack filled with sand. The plastic hull of the canoe slapped at the water again. Chalmers steadied himself by grasping the aluminum gunwales. They were cold against his hands, colder even than the body.

Chalmers looked at Edward's face in the moonlight, a round

Scott Ely

white circle in the darkness. Edward was sitting in the bow, both of his hands around the rope.

"Cut him loose!" Edward shouted.

"No!" Chalmers said.

"Chalmers?"

"No!"

"Damn you!"

The canoe bucked like a horse, sending Chalmers sprawling into the stern. His cheek was against the plastic. He felt the canoe vibrating.

He knelt and tied a rope around his father's upper body, running the rope under his arms. He tied off the rope to the stern carrying handle. He took his father's life vest in both hands. As the stern sank low in the water, the river threatened to spill over into the canoe. He had to be careful or the wire would catch them too. Then he had a hand and pulled it away from a barb. He tugged; the canoe tilted; the gunwales sank closer to the water.

"Chalmers!" Edward yelled.

Chalmers let go of the hand.

"It's no use," Edward said.

Chalmers looked at the body as Buck's light played over it. He was never going to get the barbs untangled from his father's clothes and life vest. He took the diver's knife from where he wore it strapped to the left shoulder of his life jacket and began to cut away at his father's life preserver.

"You be careful," Edward said. "His weight'll flip us if he comes loose."

Chalmers ignored him. Then the life preserver was gone, and he began cutting away at the neoprene paddling jacket. The neoprene came away in shreds. His father was wearing a light insulated vest under it and then that was gone too. He put his arms elbow-deep in the water and slashed away at his father's clothes.

"Get ready!" Chalmers yelled to Edward.

"Goddamn, we're gonna get killed!" Edward shouted.

Chalmers tugged at the naked body, but somewhere there were still barbs sunk in his father's flesh. He put his hand on the wire, taking it between the barbs. The wire vibrated in his hands with the power of the river. He shook the wire, tugging sideways at the body at the same time. Suddenly the wire went slack and with a jerk the body swung in the current behind the canoe, the left gunwale tilted, and even though he sprang to the right to balance it, the river poured into the boat.

"Cut him loose!" Edward shouted.

"No!" Chalmers said. "Get us back!"

Edward knelt in the bow, both of his hands wrapped around the rope. The rope creaked from the weight of the body which swung slowly, pendulum-like, in the current.

"I can't hold us!" Edward complained.

"You will!" Chalmers said fiercely.

"God!"

"Do it!"

Chalmers crawled over the seat and the center thwart. Then he crouched low beside Edward.

"We can do it together," Chalmers said.

"Ain't no way," Edward said. "You cut him loose."

"No!"

"Do it!"

"No."

Edward started to move toward the stern, but Chalmers blocked him with his body even though Edward was fifty pounds heavier.

"Together, Edward," Chalmers said. "Or the wire gets us."

"I always knew you was crazy, Chalmers. Just like your daddy."

Then Edward grinned.

"Reckon I'm one of you too."

Chalmers grabbed the rope, now stretched so taut that it felt like a piece of steel cable. Edward still held onto the rope threaded through the carabineer.

"Let go," Chalmers said.

Edward grabbed the rope with both hands. The weight of the body tugged at them. It was hard to hold on. They slowly began to work their way along the rope towards shore, the canoe bucking beneath them as they slipped it sideways across the current. Chalmers realized that the weight of the body, although threatening to rip the rope out of their hands, was, like an anchor, keeping the canoe stable in the current. Slowly they made their way to shore. When they crossed the eddy line into the slack water, the pressure was suddenly gone.

Chalmers stood on the rock. His cousins played their lights

over his father's body, which was marked by the barbs and a few knife cuts. His father looked very peaceful.

"Some Dobine did this," Edward said.

They were a family of commercial fishermen.

"That's right," Buck said.

"It could have been anyone," Chalmers said.

The fishermen and the paddlers were often at odds. There'd been a few incidents of kayakers caught up in trotlines. The fishermen complained that paddlers cut their lines. Until now no one had been seriously hurt.

"Like I told you," Edward said. "Dobines."

Some less successful members of that family lived nearby at Frog Eye. They existed on welfare and fished mainly to eat, not to sell.

"Don't see how we'll ever know," Buck said.

They wrapped his father's body in a plastic blanket and loaded it into Chalmers' boat. Chalmers collapsed one of the stern air bags to make space. They pulled in the barbed wire Buck had cut and took it along. They tied lines to the canoes and going along the bank walked them down to the foot of Plumb's Run.

The canoe had not handled well in the flat water as he paddled his father toward Nectar Bridge, all of them, the living and the dead, borne by the river into the heart of the spring night.

Chalmers now knelt on the foam pedestal seat, tightened the thigh straps over his legs, and buckled the chinstrap of his helmet. He sat in the eddy and tried to visualize the course in his mind, the moves he'd have to make to go through it fast. He was always fast but never quite fast enough to reach that top group of paddlers, those who won races.

So he'd always dreamed, and his father had dreamed, of designing a canoe that was quick for Chalmers, one perfectly matched to his skill at carving those smooth turns through the gates. If he could win the Nationals, he'd use the winning design to start a canoe company. They'd make roto-molded plastic boats for recreational paddlers. The nickel-plated molds needed to make them were expensive. They could invest in those only if they were assured they had a design people wanted. Those plastic boats wouldn't have the fine lines of fiberglass and Kevlar canoes, but a winning design would sell.

Now it was light enough to see the gates clearly. Patches of mist hung over the rapid, and the water was making that pulsing sound he loved.

He did some final stretches and turned the boat out of the eddy, leaning downstream, and digging hard with his paddle as he approached the first gate. Then he was through it, and he leaned back as he went over a four-foot drop so the bow wouldn't bury itself in the water and cause him to lose speed. He made his turn into the eddy smoothly and with a few paddle strokes was through the upstream gate. He crossed the eddy line and peeled out into the current, digging hard for the downstream gate on the far side of the river.

He concentrated hard, carving his turns smoothly as he worked his way down through the gates. Soon his left knee began to ache, as it always did, and his arms started to tire. He ignored the pain as he threw his whole body into every paddle stroke. Then he was through the final gate and sat in the pool below the rapid breathing hard, his body covered with sweat. He hadn't timed himself, but he knew he'd been fast. Tomorrow Livia could time him.

The sun was rising above the trees. He paddled across the pool and took the boat out of the water. As he climbed the bluff, the treetops loud with birds, he wondered if Livia had slept well.

CHAPTER FOUR

Chalmers came home to find Livia, covered with marble dust, using an electric grinder on a piece of marble. She was carving a figure of a snake, a rattler, that was almost two feet tall. The snake emerging from the stone was reared up like a cobra. It didn't seem to him that the stone could be worked in such a freestanding shape without collapsing.

"You copied that from a book?" he asked.

"No, such snakes inhabit Bankhead Lake," she said.

Livia had come upon the snakes on the hillside behind the cabin, on a trail that went up to the top of the hill. The hillside was lush and wet. The rocks were covered with green moss, and ferns grew everywhere. It reminded her of home. She had told Michael that.

"Not completely like," he said. "Somebody's raising a good crop of rattlers up there. You be careful where you put your feet and hands." She hadn't been afraid of the possibility of encountering snakes, only cautious. She'd never taken the hickory stick Michael had cut for her.

At the top she liked to climb up on a huge rock and look at the hills stretching off towards Tennessee and the big mountains. Power line pylons went up over the ridge. Far off at the edge of the ridge was a barn, its tin roof bright on clear days.

"You saw a rattler reared up like that?"

She had come upon them where the trail crossed a creek. Masses of honeysuckle grew on a hogwire fence that ran up the ridge. Michael had told her that once someone had kept hogs here. Now the hogs were gone. The sweet smell of the honeysuckle was everywhere.

On a sandy spot beside the creek they were dancing. Transfixed, she watched, taking a step closer and closer until they paused in the dance, frozen with their necks pressed against each other, their tongues flicking. An effortless flow of diamond shapes, arabesques over the sand, collapsing and then rising out of themselves. That moment was what she was trying to catch in the stone.

"Yes, it was wonderful. Two of them. A dance of love."

The snakes had dropped to the ground. One shook its bell. Michael had called the rattle a bell, and she'd laughed at that. Liked that way of talking. They slid away side by side. One disappeared into the moss-covered rocks immediately. But the other vanished slowly. She walked a little way into the rocks to watch it. The snake oozed into the rocks, its body disappearing little by little. She was close enough to hear its scales against the stone, a gentle rasping sound. She took a step, and it paused and shook its bell. It moved again, flowing not particularly fast, but smoothly into the rocks. Then it was gone.

She stood there a long time, waiting for them to return, listening to the song of unseen and unfamiliar birds, singing high in the treetops.

Chalmers knew that the snakes she'd seen weren't mating. She'd witnessed the male combat dance, perhaps a prelude to mating. His father had described the dance to Chalmers, who'd never seen it. But it was too difficult to explain all that to her.

"I make a pair," she said. "This is the first."

She turned her attention to a detail on the head. The image of them was clear in her mind, a remembrance that was more like a smell than a picture. The diamond shapes and the heads and the thick length of them all came out of sweet smell in her mind. Honeysuckle. Shapes out of a smell.

She remembered last summer when Michael had first named the vine that grew in thick masses below the cabin, next to the road where they walked in the evenings. She'd enjoyed moving in and out of that field of sweet scent. She'd locate its edges, circle around it, and then walk briskly, the dust rising in puffs under her feet, to stand in the center and breathe deeply, letting it fill her.

Chalmers imagined Livia's work must be something like carving the mold for a canoe from a block of foam, cutting away until the form the cutter had in his mind emerged. He sat on the picnic table and drank a beer. She took up the pneumatic chisel. She moved quickly about a second block, making a series of swift sure cuts, the chips falling at her feet. Livia let this snake come out of the smell of verbena. This flower grew at the house in Mobile. Through the smell she could see the moss, the water, and the snakes: elastic and golden and brown in that half light beneath the trees.

Later she sat beside him and drank a beer. The outline of the goggles and mask were on her face. He wanted to tell her that she reminded him of a raccoon and wondered if she knew the animal.

He told her what had happened to his father. And she thought of him on the river at night and the weight of the body in the canoe. She thought of her dead family and their enemies now walking through her family's house filled with beautiful things. She would tell him about the house and her family.

"Who do you think does it?" she asked.

"The sheriff doesn't think we'll ever know," he said. "All they got is that wire."

The birds, hidden in the leaves, were still singing their morning songs.

"Someone with a canoe," he said. "Had to be if it was one man. Or two men without a canoe. At that place the river is just about narrow enough to toss a rope across. Maybe someone could've done it without a boat. Pulled the wire over with a rope."

Chalmers imagined they'd used a come-along to tighten the wire.

Livia looked off into the trees.

"You forget," she said.

She thought of the house again and her sisters and brother. She saw them on the stairs, smiling and waiting for their picture to be taken. But then she thought of the prison. The images of the imagined torture were painful in their clarity. She pictured them playing soccer behind the house. And she left them there to run and laugh forever in her mind.

She would remember only the good things. But perhaps it was not possible to be selective. Perhaps everything, both good and bad, had to go. The realization of that might have been the reason she felt compelled to drown herself. Those images of her sisters at play, of Michael's hands on her breasts, would have to be replaced by a sort of even grayness in her mind. But that was also a place that held it's own terrors. She was afraid.

"No, I won't be forgetting," he said. "I want to find them stringing wire." The anger came in a great rush and left him breathless, as if he'd just finished a race.

She put her hand on his arm.

"The pistol?" she asked.

"For when that happens," he said.

"No more killing," she said. "I learn to forget. You must learn."

Chalmers was trembling. He looked into the trees on the other side of the river and recalled the feel of his father's body, that dead weight. It would be good to lay hands on whoever had strung the wire.

"I can't forgive that," Chalmers said.

"No, forget," she said. "Not forgive. Understand? You own no monopoly on despair."

He turned and looked at her.

"Listen," she said. "Listen."

Chalmers brushed some coal dust off his shirt, watching it float down to fall on the leaves that were spotted with marble dust from her clothes.

"My family are artists for generations," she said. "In Romania we have a big house. Very large. Like those on the hills of Birmingham. You have seen them?"

Birmingham was built in a bowl surrounded by hills.

"Yes," he said.

"The house is filled with art," she said. "Roman things, Etruscan masks, Greek things, paintings my father performed. It is like a museum. Ceauşescu visits us once. He looks at the things: the paintings, the statues, the tapestries, a fine head of da Vinci. He sleeps in our house and looks at it all."

"Ceauşescu?"

"A dictator. He murders my family."

"He wanted those things."

"Yes. The Securitate. The secret police. I was away in school. They forget about me."

"What happened?"

"They confess to treason. All of them die in prison. Two sisters and one brother. My parents. Tortured and killed. Because a man wants some beautiful things."

Chalmers remembered reading about the revolution in the newspaper.

"Ceaușescu is dead?" he asked.

"Yes, dead," she said. "He makes my family's house a state museum. He is the state so everything is his. He kills for beauty."

"And you?"

"My friend helps me hide from the police," she said.

She was on a train when she by chance met a friend who told her what had happened. They'd gotten off at the next stop. Her friend's father was an exporter of silk.

"I go out of the country hiding under silk."

Chalmers was confused. She saw it on his face.

"Silk in—" she began.

She searched for the right word.

"Sacks," she said. "No. Bundles."

"Bales," he offered.

She remembered how the police had searched all the trucks but hers, made the drivers unload the cargo. It had taken hours. But they had not unloaded the truck where she was hiding. Afterwards, safe in Italy, the drivers had drunk wine and laughed about it. They told her she was lucky, that she was the luckiest person in the cafe, in the town, in Italy, in the whole world. She had agreed. That was when she decided that she would learn to wait, to let herself drift, to listen for the commands of whatever it was that was protecting her. She'd learned to remain still and listen. But Michael's death was a surprise. She'd heard nothing of that from her household gods. Not a word.

"Yes," she said. "Bales. The silk is going to Italy. Over mountains. From there I go to France. To Paris. I become a political refugee."

"Now you could go back."

"No, not even if the state give me back the house and all that is in it. I never go back."

"You want to forget."

"Yes."

Chalmers recalled the look on her face when he'd first seen her in the pool. She'd been resigned to death. He'd have carried the picture of those black eyes to his grave. He imagined her walking through the big house. Something like a castle. She walking through the rooms all alone and putting her hands on the things her family had collected over the centuries. He pictured her hidden beneath bales of silk: yellow and pink and green, being carried over mountains into Italy.

"Never go back?" he asked.

"No, never," she said. "My family is dead. Nothing there. I am American."

Now she was here with this boy. She was planning on staying with him until she felt it was necessary to leave. He made her feel safe.

Chalmers thought he understood about her family. But he was the opposite. His father had set himself against his family. Things would be easier for Chalmers if he were kin to no one in the county. He thought of how simple that would be. Then there would be just the land and the river.

"I do not understand this until I jump into the river," she said. "A way of forgetting. But it is not necessary to travel so far. You remember your father and forget him all at the same time. Forget him embraced by the wire. Forget the drowned man. Forget those who killed him."

And Chalmers, begrimed with coal dust, looked at Livia, covered with marble dust, and thought of embracing her, kissing those cheeks dusted with white.

"You can win your race," she said. "Leave here. Never come back."

The words were there suddenly before her, spilling out of her mouth before she even knew they were there. It gave her a good feeling, having it happen like that.

Chalmers couldn't imagine himself leaving. He might go to South America or even to China to run difficult rivers, but always he'd return to Plumb's Bluff.

"First I've got to win," he said.

"I help you train," she said.

"That's good. But I need a faster boat. My father was working on a new design."

Later he planned to show her the female mold he was carving out of foam in the shop. His father had started the project. Now Chalmers was left to guess what his father had intended. She was a sculptor. She'd understand the problems involved.

"I help you," she said.

Chalmers wanted to make love to her right there. He ached for her. But she was so recently a widow. Surely her husband's image must be locked in her mind. Maybe that was why she kept talking about forgetting. Michael might be someone she could never forget. He didn't want her thinking of someone else. He wanted to fill her mind with nothing but Chalmers Plumb.

There had been no forgetting his mother. He had no memories of her, only pictures. Then he thought of Livia standing naked by the river. He reached out and brushed some of the white dust off her cheek, his coal-stained finger leaving a black smear.

"You won't have to go back to Romania," he said.

It frightened her, made her feel breathless to think of him killing someone with the pistol. At night on the river. She wondered what he was listening to. What voices?

"Yes," she said. "I am free. And you will have to kill no one."

Chalmers didn't reply.

He hoped she was right. The sheriff might find whoever killed Randall Plumb. But Chalmers couldn't imagine himself not wanting to take his own personal revenge on whoever had murdered his father. This was Blount County, Alabama, not Romania.

Chalmers considered how sweet it would be—once the stringers of the wire were dead—to live with Livia at Plumb's Bluff where he'd heard the ceaseless rush of the river since he was a child, smelled the pines, and felt the morning sunshine on his face as it came shooting down through the leaves of the big poplars.

CHAPTER FIVE

Chalmers walked up the steps to his grandmother's house at Susan Moore. The house was on a ridge beside the railroad tracks. It was a large two-story house, painted white, covered with lapped cypress siding. The carpenters had worked from a plan they held in their heads. They'd made bay windows, put gingerbread around the eaves, and constructed a turret room that now always leaked. He'd always heard that the wrap-around porch had been his great-great-grandmother's idea. And the coal scuttles. She'd had a different colored tile installed in the hearth of each one. He remembered Sunday afternoons spent on that porch when he was a child, the cypress boards cool against his legs. He'd walk the porch rail, bordered by huge azalea bushes. Sometimes he'd walked it with his eyes closed, his arms spread out like a pair of wings for balance. He'd never fallen. In the spring, when the bushes were in bloom, he sometimes wanted to fall, had imagined falling down through the bushes amid a shower of brilliant red flowers.

His grandmother had asked him to come see her. Edward, who had brought the message, hadn't even gotten out of his truck. Livia was working. As they talked Edward kept staring at her, but he didn't ask any questions.

"A pretty woman," Edward said.

Livia was covered with sweat. It had cut tracks in the marble dust, revealing the dark skin beneath.

"Prettier than most," Chalmers said.

Then Edward drove off.

The town was a single line of stores, most of them vacant. There was still a post office run by one of Chalmers' cousins and a store where you could buy gas and groceries. Six big houses like his grandmother's were on a ridge on one side of the railroad tracks, stores on the other, and behind them a collection of small bungalows. Three of the big houses were boarded up. A school teacher and his mother, the daughter of the owner of the defunct hardware store, who five years before had committed suicide, lived in the closest one. In the other two were the widows of the bank president and the druggist. No black people lived in the town or the county. The soil had been too poor for the plantation system and the people too poor to own slaves. There had been no town at all until after the Civil War when the railroad came through. Until then people grew a little corn to make whiskey and to feed their cattle and hogs and hunted and fished.

The town had briefly boomed during World War II because of a nearby army camp. And after the war, when the veterans had come home, the bungalows behind the stores had been built. A factory came that made electric irons. It failed. Then during the Vietnam War a company moved into the building outside of town that had housed the iron factory. There people from the county found work assembling fuses for mortar shells. After the war was over, the people gave up on the town and moved to Birmingham.

The house was built only a few yards away from the railroad tracks. Chalmers' great-great-grandfather had been a frustrated railroad man. He'd come home from World War I intending to work for the railroad, but instead he'd gone to work for his father in the lumber business. He'd never escaped to the railroad. That was why Chalmers thought his grandfather had built the house so close to the tracks. Amory Plumb liked the sound of trains.

But to Chalmers that sound had been a source of terror. As a child he'd been afraid to sleep in his grandmother's house. He'd awake in the night to the roar of the freight that sounded as if it were going to come right through the wall of his bedroom. The whole house vibrated. His appeals for help were lost, his screams carried away by the violence and enormity of the train's passing. Then the whole house would be quiet again as the train rumbled away in the distance, the engineer blowing the whistle one last time as the locomotive approached the highway crossing just outside of town. And Chalmers lay covered with the sweat of fear, listening to the sound of his father's snoring from the room next door. He was always glad when he and his father returned to

Plumb's Bluff.

A squirrel barked at him from the big oak next to the house. Chalmers looked up into the tree. It was another one of his cousins, imitating a squirrel.

"John David," Chalmers shouted.

High overhead a limb of the oak shook and John David lowered himself out of the oak tree. John David, dressed in camouflage, came down fast. He was wearing a purple climbing harness and rode a green mountain climbing rope, marked with a yellow stripe, down out of the tree.

"John David," Grandmother Rosa yelled. "Thirty seconds."

John David grinned at Chalmers. Then he dug his climbing irons into the oak and scrambled up the trunk. Chalmers didn't think a squirrel could have done it any quicker. John David walked across a limb and disappeared through the window of Grandmother Rosa's room.

Chalmers went into the house and started up the staircase to the second floor. Grandmother Rosa had ordered John David enough mountaineering equipment to make an ascent of Everest, but John David used it only on trees. He'd been to the top of every tall tree in the county. He was fearless and had never fallen.

When Chalmers walked into his grandmother's room, he saw John David reaching out to move a piece on a chessboard. It was his grandfather's doing. Other men had brought home weapons or, if they were lucky, gold or diamonds they'd looted, but his grandfather, after walking all the way across France to Germany, had brought home the knowledge of the game of chess. And he'd looted something tangible, a chess board with a set of carved ivory pieces. There were Gothic knights and stern kings and queens. His grandfather had found them just after he'd crossed the Rhine. Chalmers imagined his grandfather's war-grimed hands opening drawers and cabinets in a deserted house. Then his grandfather had carried that set in his rucksack all the way across Germany. It was not until he reached Berlin that he'd learned to play. A woman in a brothel had taught him the game.

John David's parents, drunk most of the time, had all but abandoned him. Then they'd died of TB and Grandmother Rosa had taken him into her house. It was before she'd known about his ability at chess. She'd done it simply because he was kin and no one else had offered. Some people thought John David belonged in the state mental hospital. But Grandmother Rosa had allowed him to stay on at Susan Moore.

"I'm used to his game," she liked to say. "We're used to each other."

John David had stopped talking the day his mother was buried. Grandmother Rosa had carried him to a doctor in Birmingham, and several weeks later he'd beaten one of the nurses at a game of chess. Then he beat the psychiatrist. They thought they had a prodigy on their hands until the fatal mechanical aspect of his game was revealed by the best player in Alabama.

Chalmers had never heard John David say a word, but his father said he'd once heard him having a conversation with Grandmother Rosa. John David, Chalmers guessed, was about forty now but still had the lean body of a young man. For years Grandmother Rosa had taken John David to the psychiatrist in Birmingham in an attempt to turn John David into an ordinary person. That had failed. John David refused to talk. She'd tried him in the mine office, but he'd wander off in the middle of some task she'd assigned him. So now all John David did was play chess and climb trees. And Grandmother Rosa talked to him, enough for both of them. She'd go on and on, and John David would never say a word in reply. Maybe when they were alone he did?

John David moved a pawn. He reset the clock and went out the window again and into the tree. He went up fast, going quickly all the way to the top, stopping only when he feared that the limbs could no longer support his weight. Sometimes he did consider what would happen if he fell, but although he could imagine himself falling, he could never imagine himself hitting the ground. It would be like a dream of falling from which he'd always awake before he hit.

John David looked toward the river. He couldn't see it, but he could see the top of the ridge that formed one side of its gorge. It was a river that flowed in his dreams.

Miss Rosa had told him she wanted the coal beneath her son's land. She talked to him while they played chess, thinking, he supposed, that he didn't listen to much of what she said. Or maybe she thought that he didn't understand everything. Like a child. She might have talked the same way to a dog or a cat.

"He wasn't killed in Vietnam," she said. "I could hardly sleep at night thinking about him being killed. And he survived that and came home and did nothing with that land, nothing."

She'd said that more than once. And John David had looked at Randall Plumb when he saw him at the store at the crossroads or at the grocery store in Blountsville, and it appeared to John David that man was alive only by accident. John David had stood close to him so that he could smell the cigars he carried in his pocket and the scent of coal dust and another smell, which John David thought was dynamite. It was as if his being alive was some sort of mistake, an oversight. He should be buried at the church. Miss Rosa should have the coal.

Then he began to dream of the river, of that narrow spot in the gorge where Randall ran his canoe. Everyone knew he ran his boat at Plumb's Run on moonlit nights. Where most people were reluctant to go in the daytime. He was famous for that throughout the county. Most often he did it by the light of the full moon, but there were stories of him doing it on starless and moonless winter nights when the cliff faces that rose above Plumb's Run were covered with icicles and snow lay in patches beneath the pines. No one could live long in that cold water. But the dream told him nothing. It was just of the water, penned up by the boulders, going fast, its darkness churned to white by the violence of its passage.

The dream persisted, and he went to look at Plumb's Run, that section he'd never seen but had heard Miss Rosa talk about. He was crossing a barbed wire fence and had snagged his pants leg on the wire when he saw clearly what he should do. It was like the solution to a chess problem, something he had hardly to think about. He went down to the river through the oaks and pines to look at the rapid.

As he squatted on a rock, only a few feet away from the water, feeling the power of it as it surged and pulsed against the rocks, he remembered Miss Rosa's fear (he had heard her say it many times) that one night her son would end up drowned at this rapid. She would be without blame, without sin. Not even Brother Sprott at church would blame her. Or God. John David had been surprised that he wasn't concerned about God. He sat there a long time and studied the rapid, considering where to place the wire.

Then, on a night of the full moon, he'd gone down to the rapids. He tied a line to a rock, attached at one end to a brand new coil of wire he'd stolen from out of the back of a neighbor's pickup at the crossroads store, and threw it across. Then he went upstream and stood on the bank of a deep pool and looked at the expanse of dark water for a long time. He couldn't swim. He found a driftwood log. After taking off his clothes and making a bundle of them and placing them carefully in a fork on the log, he swam the river, holding tightly to the log and kicking himself across. The cold water had taken his breath away.

On the bank he sat on a rock and shook himself like a dog. The air was warm enough that he didn't bother putting his clothes back on. He was just going to have to take them off again to swim the river. He made his way down through the rhododendron thickets to the center of the rapid.

He pulled the wire across just as the moon rose above the cliff, bathing the rapid in its cold light. It was difficult getting it as tight as he wished, but its sag did tend to hide it in the water. He took up a stick and twisted the wire around it in an attempt to take up the slack. As the water surged against the wire, it glinted in the moonlight, but he knew that Randall Plumb wouldn't see it, not from where he knelt in his canoe. It would catch him, and he would drown. Miss Rosa would have the coal.

He swam the river again and hid behind a rock and watched the approach to the rapid. It didn't seem to him that he had waited a long time before he saw Randall Plumb appear in the long pool above the rapid. He was smoking a cigar, the tip glowing in the darkness. He took the boat into an eddy just above the rapid. Then the cigar went out, and a moment later John David saw him, illuminated by the moonlight, swing the boat out into the current and go down into the rapid.

John David, from his perch in the oak, looked at the ridge and thought of Randall Plumb hanging on the wire. John David felt neither fear of discovery nor guilt. That night on the river he'd felt no connection between his stringing the wire and Randall's death. In his mind the wire had become a natural part of the river, no different from one of those undercut boulders.

Chalmers looked at the board.

"You're gonna lose your queen," he said.

"Hush," Grandmother Rosa said.

Chalmers saw check in three moves. It was no wonder that John David was out playing on the tree.

She studied the board carefully. Chalmers thought he'd try something with the knight to hold off the bishop that would threaten the queen. But it was all useless. The game was over, and she knew it.

Instead she moved a pawn. It was a move that would only delay the final outcome. She turned to Chalmers and asked him to sit down. He took John David's stool. He noticed that she hadn't reset the timer.

"He won't know if it's been a minute or six hours," she said. "How do you think that feels?"

"I don't know," Chalmers said.

"I've often wondered," she said. "I suppose it would be like I was a child again. Not exactly like. But close."

"I guess."

He wasn't interested in having a conversation with her about John David and knew she wasn't either. He wished she'd get to the point.

"Chalmers, I want to talk with you about the land," she said.

"I promised," Chalmers said. "I don't—"

She held up her hand for silence, and he stopped.

"Deathbed promises," she said. "Your father could've stopped the whole crazy business, but he didn't. I nursed Mitchell right here in this room. He was out of his head most of the time. He was like that when he talked with Randall."

"I promised."

She looked down at the board, appearing to study John David's various options.

"Who is this girl?" she asked.

"Someone I met on the river," he said.

"Where is she from?"

"Romania."

John David stuck his head in the window.

"Not yet," she said.

She waved her hand at him. John David grinned and went straight up as if he were a spider attached to a strand of silk.

"Chalmers, you're not going to do a thing with that land," she said. "I'll give you a good price."

Chalmers shook his head.

"And a share of the profits."

"No, ma'am."

"You could use the money to train. That's what you've needed. Time to train."

Chalmers thought of his father's promise to his father, and now he had promised his own father. If he had a son, he'd make him promise.

"There's been too much promising to go back on it," he said.

"I understand," she said. "But you think about it."

Chalmers imagined the coal lying under the rock and dirt. Tons and tons of Pocahontas coal. A huge black slab of it lying under the overburden.

"And you need to stop looking for whoever killed Randall," she said. "Let the sheriff handle it."

Chalmers recalled what Livia had told him.

"He's not looking hard enough," Chalmers said.

"What will you do if you find them?" she asked. "Shoot them with that pistol. Then you'll go to prison. Leave it to the sheriff."

"My father is dead. I might end up in jail, but he'll rest easy."

"I don't care if you kill them. But even if you don't go to prison, think about what you'll feel like."

Chalmers didn't think it would do anything to him.

"They won't be stringing any more wire," he said. "Daddy will rest easy."

"Yes," she said. "You'll be alive. Think about that."

"All I can think about is how good it's going to feel to know they're dead."

"Leave it to the sheriff."

"I can't."

John David had appeared at the windowsill, dangling on the rope. The rope creaked. He slowly turned until his back was to them. The purple harness was brilliant against his camouflage.

"Your father and I never got along," she said. "I didn't want that. He didn't either. It just happened. I wanted it to be some other way. Many times I've sat in this room and cried over Randall. I lost him."

Because you wanted the land, he thought.

"I fought with Brother Sprott to get him buried right," she said. "We could've buried him in Birmingham. I'd have paid for a plot. Paid some preacher to say words over him."

"He's fine where he is. It's good enough for other Plumbs."

"It's not the church graveyard. No words were said over him. I worry about his soul."

Chalmers considered telling her he didn't believe in souls.

That the words he'd said were sufficient. But there was no need for that. He had no desire to make his grandmother suffer.

"He's fine," he said. "He's at a pretty place."

Chalmers considered how peaceful it was under the pines. You could hear the river but not the traffic on the highway bridge.

"I think Vietnam made him crazy," she said. "Mitchell came home like that. But he got over it. Randall didn't. He put his craziness on you. He didn't mean to do it. But it happened. Don't you see. You know he wouldn't want you out on the river with that pistol."

"I won't change my mind," he said. "I'm sorry."

"About the coal or the pistol?" she asked.

"Both."

"Don't you shoot anyone. You promise me. Take them to the sheriff if you catch them."

"I'll do what I have to do."

It wasn't that he hadn't considered what it might be like to catch someone stringing wire in the moonlight. It might well turn out to be one of his neighbors, someone who once sat next to him at church.

And he thought of what selling the land would mean. Strip mining changed the land in grotesque ways. Eventually pines would gain a hold on it, but there were pockets of toxic spoil where nothing would ever grow. And even if the vegetation came back the shape of the land was forever changed. Hills you'd looked at all your life were reduced in a few months to shallow depressions. The spill silted up nearby creeks and rivers.

He was helping Rudy Blount do it to land someone had sold, sold and gone off to live at Panama City where they'd sit in a condo and stare out at that blue water and white sand every day of their lives.

"You be careful around that girl," she said. "Who knows what she wants?"

"She's a sculptor," he said.

"Young girls don't know what they are."

Chalmers supposed that Grandmother Rosa would laugh at any opinion he had about that, so he decided to say nothing. Right now he wished he were sitting on the picnic table and watching Livia work on a piece of marble. The way the image appeared in his mind so easily took him by surprise.

"She's just a friend," he said.

"You think about that land," she said. "We know the coal is there. You'd never have to set another charge."

She walked to the window.

"Thirty seconds," she yelled.

The branches shook above the window, and John David dropped down on the rope. He sat on the windowsill and grinned at them. The climbing irons strapped to his legs made him look as if he were wearing braces. He walked across the room and studied the board.

"You bring that girl for dinner Sunday," she said.

"Yes, ma'am," he said.

"Brother Sprott will be there. I want you to make peace with him."

"I've had enough of preachers," he said.

"Come and be polite," she said.

Chalmers said he would. He thought of looking at Brother Sprott's thin white face across the table.

"Check," John David said in a high-pitched voice.

Chalmers had always imagined that his voice would be deeper.

It was the first word that Chalmers had ever heard him say. Chalmers looked at the board. John David had done in two moves what Chalmers believed would have taken at least five. He wondered what it meant that John David had spoken in his presence. Maybe, he thought, Grandmother Rosa was carrying John David down to the psychiatrist in Birmingham again.

John David pressed the time clock. Then he was gone again out the window to continue his ceaseless climbing about the oak.

"You can never tell about John David," she said. "You remember on Sunday. You bring that girl."

"Yes, ma'am," he said.

Somehow she didn't seem to be old enough to be his grandmother. It was as if there was something of John David in her. He thought of her swinging on one of those brightly colored ropes. She could do it.

Then Chalmers went out of the room and down the stairs, his hand running along the dark mahogany banister. Outside in the yard John David began barking at him like a squirrel.

Chalmers ignored him.

John David barked again.

Chalmers wondered if Grandmother Rosa and John David sometimes had lengthy conversations.

John David made a new sound, one that was neither human nor animal. Chalmers' father had called it John David's yowl.

Chalmers knew John David was agitated. Pretty soon he'd do something, maybe disappear into the woods along the river for three or four days and everyone would be out hunting him. Then Grandmother Rosa would have to carry him back down to Birmingham for a few sessions.

A yowl again came from the treetop. This time the pitch was higher than usual. Chalmers looked up to him and waved. John David didn't wave back. Chalmers turned and walked quickly to the truck and did not look back.

John David considered Chalmers' patrols of Plumb's Run. If Chalmers died then there would be no one to take his place. The coal would become Miss Rosa's. He considered what would happen if Chalmers caught him stringing wire. He knew about the .44 Chalmers carried with him. This time it would be different. Chalmers was looking for the wire.

He decided to wait for the dreams of the rapids to begin again. One night he'd close his eyes and suddenly he'd be filled with the sound of the rapids: he'd feel the mist on his skin; he'd smell the wet rocks. Then he'd string the wire, pull it tight in some place where Chalmers could not escape. He imagined the wire not as a single strand this time but as a web. He'd take a come-along with him to pull it tight. And he'd make a raft of logs to support his tools. He imagined himself walking naked along the bank, the rhododendron leaves a soft carpet beneath his feet.

The river would sweep Chalmers into the steel web. Miss Rosa would have the coal.

CHAPTER SIX

Chalmers stood next to Rudy Blount. They were waiting for Chalmers to set off charges in the overburden. Once it had been broken into pieces and the dragline had removed it, they could get at the deposit of coal beneath. The right trouser leg of Rudy's suit was grimed with coal dust. Rudy had knelt to examine a broken bulldozer tread. Chalmers was covered with coal dust, mixed with the reddish clay of the overburden.

Behind them was the trailer Rudy used as the mine office. Off by itself, three hundred yards away, was the small portable building that served as Chalmers' blasting shack where he stored explosives and other equipment. Ahead of them was a clear area where the ground had been scraped clean by the dragline that pulled out the coal. This ended at the place where Chalmers had set charges in the overburden, in a cliff face perhaps forty feet high. Off behind the trailer was a steep artificial ridge created by the overburden the dump trucks had hauled out of the mine. Now they were waiting for Chalmers to blast again and break up the overburden. Everything: men, machines, the buildings, the scrub oak they still grew on the overburden—not worth the trouble of cutting even for firewood—was covered with a layer of coal dust.

But Rudy wasn't ready for Chalmers to blast yet. He wanted to talk.

Rudy was complaining that his private bridge had been washed out by the winter floods. The bridge rested on the old foundations of the first bridge built across the river in the county. It happened every year, and every year he built it back so he'd have quicker access to a pasture where he raised cattle. Chalmers always wondered how Rudy managed to run the strip mining company and not lose his shirt in competition with Grandmother Rosa when he seemed to spend most of his time worrying about the bridge.

Chalmers expected that Rudy was about the same age as Grandmother Rosa. At one time people thought they might marry, but then there was a dispute over a piece of land and that was the end of their going to Birmingham every weekend for dinner and dancing. Rudy sent her flowers. He grew roses on the piece of land where he kept cattle. Once he had the bridge completed and proven against the winter floods, Rudy planned to build a house on a ridge above the river bottom.

"Making the garden first," Rudy liked to say. "Then the house. Won't look like a subdivision house. Folks'll think it's been there a hundred years."

Chalmers could recall smelling roses in Grandmother Rosa's house. One week Rudy had sent her a dozen roses every day. Yellow, pink, coral, red. Every color you could think of.

Rudy looked much older than Grandmother Rosa. Chalmers tried to imagine them dancing in Birmingham. Rudy was a big man but quick on his feet. He was said to be a good dancer. His face was beginning to collapse around his cheekbones, the skin hanging in loose folds. Chalmers had never seen him when he wasn't dressed in a coat and tie.

"That Row-manian girl still out there with you?" Rudy asked.

"Yes, sir," Chalmers said.

"Row-mania," Rudy said. "That's where vampires come from. You believe in vampires, Chalmers?"

"No, sir," Chalmers said.

"Neither do I," Rudy said.

Burl Wise, the foreman at the mine, walked over to them.

Chalmers thought of Livia carving marble. When he'd finished his morning run, she'd already been at work.

"You ready, Chalmers?" Burl asked.

Chalmers had spent the morning setting the charges in a cut, an eighty by three hundred foot section of ground.

"Fire in the hole!" Chalmers yelled.

The cry was repeated across the mine.

Chalmers pressed a button on the battery-operated blasting machine to obtain a voltage reading on the wires. He wanted to make sure none of the wires were grounded. Charges that didn't go off were a dangerous nuisance. He'd drilled the holes down through the rock and clay to the coal, backfilled them a couple of feet, and refilled the hole with ammonium nitrate mixed with a little diesel fuel. Then he'd primed the hole with a stick of dynamite in which he'd inserted a blasting cap. The forty charges he'd set were connected to detonation cord with delays built into it so the charges would go off sequentially. If they all went off at once, they'd shatter the windows in the trailers and farmhouses near the mine.

"Fire in the hole!" he yelled.

He pressed the fire button on the blasting machine. The sequential charges went off, the ground rippling in that weird sort of way it always did. Black smoke and dust rose from the cut. They used ammonium nitrate—fertilizer—instead of dynamite because it was cheaper and safer to handle. Also the explosion itself occurred more slowly than with dynamite and so tended to pulverize the rock, making it easier to remove.

"I'm using steel this year," Rudy was saying to Burl. "And I'm raising the piers by six feet. I won't get washed out again."

"Less there's a big flood," Burl said. "That river can jump right out of its banks."

The machines moved in to clear away the rubble and reach the coal beneath. Chalmers began setting charges in another cut. He was drilling holes when Burl came over in his pickup.

"You come see what we found," Burl said.

Chalmers went with Burl and walked down into the depression the machines had carved out. Most of the rock was gone and there was Black Creek grade coal beneath their feet.

The men had dismounted from their machines and were looking at a cliff of white stone at the end of the cut. Rudy Blount was standing at the foot of it.

"What's that?" Chalmers asked.

"Marble," Burl said. "Why, we must have got ourselves moved to Georgia."

Here was the marble he'd told Livia didn't exist in North Alabama. It was pure white, like a snow bank. A snow bank in May in Alabama. Rudy stood at the cliff face, running his hand over the stone.

"I'm gonna go in the tombstone business," Rudy said.

They all laughed.

Chalmers picked his way through the sharp-edged boulders to the base of the cliff. The marble rose shining above them. He had no idea how deep it was, but he doubted it went far. A freak formation. He ran his hands over the rock.

"Chalmers, you get busy and blast this out of here," Rudy said. "Why, I may use this stuff for my bridge footers. Only marble bridge in Blount County. Flood proof."

Rudy laughed.

"You hear me, Chalmers," Rudy said. "You take this stuff out of here in blocks. You can do it. You're just like your daddy. A genius with dynamite."

"It'll take awhile," Chalmers said.

"Do it," Rudy said. "I don't care how damn long it takes."

"Yes, sir," Chalmers said.

Rudy picked up a piece of marble and turned it over in his hands.

"You gonna sell your land to your Grandmother Rosa?" Rudy asked.

"No," Chalmers said.

"She asked?"

Chalmers looked up at the wall of marble.

"Just like she asked my daddy," Chalmers said.

"I'll make you a better price," Rudy said. "If you ever decide."

Rudy walked off with Burl, leaving Chalmers to contemplate how he was going to blast out chunks of marble. He decided he'd use lengths of det cord and drop it into holes drilled into the stone.

The marble was a pure white with veins of rose running through it. He tried to imagine a piece of it shaped into one of Livia's figures. The marble she was using was a darker stuff. It didn't seem right that toothed and fanged figures should emerge out of that snowy whiteness. Or that it be used as footers for Rudy Blount's bridge. It seemed to him the marble should be carved into the curved soft shapes of men and women like he'd seen in picture books on art.

He drilled the holes and set the charges. When he pressed the button of the blasting machine, a block of marble dropped neatly off the face of the cliff. All afternoon he repeated the process and worked beyond quitting time to finish the job. As it turned out, the deposit of marble was not large. He'd only cut twenty-one blocks, to a depth of about thirty feet, when he hit rock again.

Then he was done. He looked at the white blocks as they lay jumbled about amid the black coal and the gray shale, like the playthings of some giant child. Burl drove up in his truck.

"Rudy'll want to give you overtime," Burl said.

"He'll do me right," Chalmers said.

"I hope you find them that killed your daddy," Burl said.

"Thanks," Chalmers said.

"I got me a forty-five you can have," Burl said.

"Daddy had a pistol," Chalmers said.

Chalmers remembered his talks with Livia and his grandmother. Burl approved of what he was doing. Rudy Blount would approve.

Burl surveyed the blocks of marble.

"How do you suppose that marble got in here?" Burl asked.

"You'll have to ask Brother Sprott about things like that," Chalmers said.

He was eager to get home and tell Livia about the marble.

Burl laughed.

"Or a geologist from the University?"

"Take your pick."

"Brother Sprott was wrong about your daddy. I voted against it."

"Thanks."

"Seems to me Randall's got him a better place. The Lord ain't on the lookout for preacher's words over every dead person."

"That's what I think."

"Sheriff's going all over the county asking about who's been buying barbed wire."

"Doing his job."

"Chalmers, I'd keep my eye on them Dobines. Pick Dobine especially. He could do it. Didn't like your daddy setting poles in the river. Attracted city folks. Says they cut his lines. That man don't like nobody."

Chalmers had run into Pickens Dobine on the river just before Christmas. Pick had a freshly cut Christmas tree in the bow of a battered aluminum canoe. He was camped on some flat rocks below one of the falls, frying ham in an iron skillet. It had been a bright but very cold day with patches of snow on the ground.

Chalmers was running the river to see the icicles, which grew to be longer than a man, on the cliff face at Skirum Bluff.

He remembered Pick complaining about paddlers cutting his trotlines and how he liked the river in the winter when few people ran it. Chalmers wondered if Pick knew how to ferry a canoe across the swift current of a rapid like Plumb's Run. He'd never seen Pick in the canoe again. Maybe by now he'd sold it.

"If I was the sheriff, I'd go out to Pick's and see if some coils of wire are laying about," Burl said.

"Maybe he will," Chalmers said.

"You want me to go with you, I will."

Chalmers imagined how the .44 would feel in his hand. And what would they do if they found coils of wire? If Pick had done it, he'd have to be crazy to leave coils of wire lying about. Pick had nothing to fence. He didn't even keep chickens. Chalmers remembered what Livia had told him about forgetting. Even Burl, who was not kin, hadn't forgotten. Why should he?

"Let the sheriff do it," Chalmers said.

"Yeah, I suppose he's already been out there," Burl said. "Probably the first place he looked. I just wanted to help, Chalmers."

Chalmers thanked Burl and then put away his supplies in the blasting shack. Burl left and Chalmers locked the gate to the mine. It was growing dark; bats twisted in the air overhead. He looked out over the wasteland. The scent of some flower tree mixed with the smell of coal dust and diesel fuel. And off across the barren ground the blocks of marble glowed in the gathering darkness, their shapes shifting in the fading light.

CHAPTER SEVEN

Chalmers went home and told Livia about the snowy white marble and what Rudy Blount planned to do with it. Livia was surprised that the appearance of the marble made her uneasy. He had said that no such marble existed. Then suddenly it was there. Just as the Securitate let no one escape, but she had escaped. The marble was just like her friend on the train. And the silk. She remembered how long she'd lain under the bales, inside the little wooden box they'd constructed for her, and listened to the voices of the border guards. Later she believed she would feel easy about the appearance of the stone.

"Good," she said. "I will look at it on a later day."

"We could go tomorrow," he said.

"No, later."

He decided to leave her alone. Besides, the stone belonged to Rudy.

They took coffee out to the picnic table. A string of naked light bulbs was suspended from a wire. A group of moths circled about them. The rush of the river rose up to them over the lip of the bluff. Livia looked tired. She had a cut across the back of her hand.

"I have much work," she said. "I need no new marble now."

She liked the sound of that. When her work was finished, more white marble would appear. She imagined Chalmers blasting at the mine one day and uncovering another deposit, startling white amid the coal. Chalmer's excitement over the marble at the mine was unsettling. He wanted it to be something unusual. She desperately wanted it to be not unusual at all, a further confirmation of the way she'd decided to live her life.

Chalmers was disappointed. He'd thought they'd go to the mine in the morning and take a look at it before Rudy had it hauled off for his bridge. Except for the snakes, she'd kept making the same sort of figure over and over out of that dark marble. The white kind could be used for something new.

"It's like a snow bank," he said.

She laughed.

"I have seen much marble," she said.

"Not like this," he said. "What would you make with it?"

Livia shrugged.

"I have other figures to make."

Chalmers thought of the toothed figures, the stark geometrical shapes. Maybe she would make nothing else the rest of her life. At least she wasn't making those composite creatures, nightmares you could touch.

"You will show me the river tomorrow?" she asked.

She wanted no more talk of the marble. She'd been wanting to go out on the river with him.

The next day was Saturday. Chalmers had planned to spend it working on the mold for the new boat.

"I've got to finish the mold," he said.

He'd given Livia a tour of the shop and explained about the mold and different kinds of layups. He'd lay the resin-soaked cloth into the mold, building up the hull of the canoe in layers. The mold's shape was graceful but slightly asymmetrical. The portion of the boat behind the paddler's seat was slightly wider than the front. That shape was necessary to make it go through the water faster.

"In the morning you work," she said. "In the afternoon we will view the river."

"We can do that," he said.

He knew his willingness to take her was partly because of his problems with the mold. If he knew the solution, the right cuts to make, he'd have spent every hour of the weekend on it.

"You teach me to paddle a canoe?" she asked.

"Sure," he said.

He thought she'd learn quickly. He'd seen the muscles in her arms when she'd brought the marble blocks up out of the pool at Nectar Bridge.

"I am strong," she said.

"Yes," he said.

"You teach me the gates."

He laughed.

"Later," he said. "You'll have to learn to paddle first."

"I will learn," she said.

He left her at the table.

Chalmers spent the morning working on the mold. He had the feeling he was making a boat that would not perform well. And instead of solving the problems of design, he found himself slipping off in reveries of Livia. He tried not to think of her but instead concentrate on the lines of the boat. Instead of a breast there was the way the sides flared slightly; instead of the curve of her leg there was the curve of the boat's hull line. But it was useless. He put aside his tools and sat cross-legged on the concrete floor, studying the mold that rested on two sawhorses.

Outside he heard the sound of Livia's tools as she attacked the marble. He imagined that she had no trouble making decisions; she knew exactly what she was about.

Livia opened the door of the shop. She wouldn't come in because she was covered with marble dust. "So clean you can eat off the floor," he'd said. She hadn't understood at first but laughed after he'd explained.

"I finish," she said.

Chalmers told her that he was coming. After they returned he'd work some more on the mold.

Together they carried the tandem plastic canoe down the trail to the water. It was the same canoe he'd used to take his father home.

They launched the boat at the pool below the rapid. A couple of paddlers were practicing on Chalmers' course. He put Livia in the bow and told her to sit still. Then they went down the river.

Livia looked up at the new-leaved trees, which formed an arch over the river. They were going through a flat, shallow section, the banks low on either side. Occasionally the canoe scraped against rocks. Everywhere the water was white.

"A rock garden," Chalmers said.

She liked the sound.

"A garden of stone," she said.

And then she thought of where her family was buried, in the cemetery next to the village church. It was a peaceful thought. She imagined her sculptures set in the shoal, the water foaming about them as it did the dark rocks.

Now the river formed a deep pool and the banks were high and covered with bushes that bore big white flowers. On one side was a cliff face. The pool ended at a jumble of big boulders where the plane of the water disappeared. There was the sound of falling water.

"Hold on," Chalmers said.

As she took hold of the gunwales, cold against her hands, she thought of those ancient mapmakers whose maps depicted the point where the flat world ended. Ships were always poised on the brink of the void. She heard the sound of Chalmers' paddle in the water and felt him shift his weight. As they went past the boulders and over the drop, she saw a large snake, its body banded with red and yellow, coiled on one of the rocks. It never moved as they went past. They went down over the three-foot drop, the canoe hitting the bottom with a bump and water splashing in her face. Chalmers was laughing. As he swung the canoe around, she looked for the snake on the rock. It was gone. She wondered if it had been there at all.

"A snake," she said.

Chalmers laughed.

"Banded water snake," he said. "Not a moccasin. Harmless."

Now the river was a long pool with smaller drops. He asked her to take up the paddle. He showed her various strokes: draws, cross draws, prys, and backstrokes. They practiced stopping the boat in an eddy. He had her kneel for that. From the stern he drove the boat across the eddyline and into the eddy. She reached out and dug her paddle in the water, and the canoe swung around and then they were pointed upstream. The boat rocked gently in the turbulence of the eddy.

"Good," he said. "Good."

She glanced back at him and smiled.

"A beautiful river, Chalmers," she said.

"Yes," he said.

Chalmers looked at the tree-covered banks and wondered how his father could have been murdered amid such beauty. It was going to be impossible to forget his father's murder. He didn't think she'd forgotten what had happened to her family in Romania.

They went over a four-foot drop. Livia had the paddle in her hands and braced the boat, using the paddle as an outrigger as he had instructed her. She got a little wet. The water on her black hair sparkled in the sunlight.

Then in the pool below the rapid, he turned the canoe up into the Blackburn Fork. This was a good-sized tributary of the river. They'd paddle upstream and then later in the day float back down. There were no rapids, only a series of small shoals. If they were lucky they'd see deer or wild turkey.

At the first shoal he spotted an otter crossing the river with a fish in its mouth.

"Lutra," Livia said.

She pointed at the animal. It glanced at them as it reached the bank and disappeared.

"Lutra," she said.

"Otter," he said.

"Otter," she said. "Otter."

"They have a mud slide around the bend."

"Mud slide?"

"Yes, they slide on their bellies down the bank. I've seen 'em do it a few times. But you have to be real quiet."

Chalmers eased the canoe around the bend, careful to make no splashes with the paddle. He saw the slide. The mud glistened in the sunlight. The otters had been using it recently.

"I slide with them," she said.

She shucked off her clothes and stood up. Chalmers had little time to admire her breasts and legs. He was busy bracing the canoe with a paddle face laid flat against the water so that the boat wouldn't overturn.

"They slide with me," Livia said.

She went over the side. The water was not as cold as she'd expected. She opened her eyes and looked for the otters, but she could see nothing. The water was not as clear as at the Nectar Bridge pool. She surfaced.

A childhood memory was with her, of swimming in a river bordered by grassy fields. She resisted it for a moment, fearful it might lead to memories of the terrible past, but then she gave herself up to the pleasant memories, hoping no unpleasant ones would intrude. Large black birds flew against a blue sky. They had been having a picnic on the banks. It was a very hot day. Her mother had stripped off her clothes and dived into the pool. Her heavy breasts quivered as she gathered her body for the dive and then she was gone, her white body disappearing into the dark water. Livia felt her own small breasts. She was envious of her mother's breasts. Her sisters, younger than she, whose chests were hardly different from a boy's, laughed and followed their mother into the water.

She dived into the pool. Her mother taught them all how to float on their backs. Livia spread her arms and drifted in the water, borne downstream by the gentle current, watching the white clouds float across a blue sky. Now the black birds were gone. There were just the clouds against the sky. She floated close to her mother, listening to the sound of her talk and laughter. She was telling them how they caught fish with nets in the river. Livia imagined a net filled with silver-sided fish. She imagined the men straining to pull it out of the water.

They floated into a pool, their bodies swinging in slow circles in the current. Livia smelled the scent of manure. A cow bellowed. A human voice yelled and then another. The voices faded away and all was still again. The clouds drifted silently across the blue sky.

Her mother called, telling the girls to look, otters were in the pool. She was laughing. Livia raised her head and let her legs sink. The water was colder deeper down. The first thing she saw was an otter staring at her, a grave but at the same time curious, expression on its face. Then another otter appeared and another and another, a whole family of otters. Led by their mother the girls played with them, sometimes on the surface and sometimes underwater. Livia imitated their swimming, turning her body over and over in the water. She wanted to pet one, but they always stayed just out of reach.

All at once the otters were gone. She and her mother and her sisters swam and waded back upstream. They lay on the blanket that held the picnic and let their bodies dry in the sun. All around them the grass rose, green and succulent in the heat, clouds of midges swarming over it. Livia remembered the scent of her sisters' wet hair drying in the sun. She'd considered how an otter's wet fur might smell as one of the animals lay on a midstream rock, basking in the sun. She wondered if it was going to be possible on this river, with this boy close by, to immerse herself in a past that was only beautiful and sweet.

Chalmers' voice took her out of her reverie.

"They won't come close to us," he said.

Livia swam for the bank and took hold of a tree root. The slide was to her left. Chalmers sculled the canoe across the pool toward her. She climbed out of the water and started picking her way up the slick clay bank. She liked the feel of the clay beneath her bare feet. The bank was covered with otter tracks.

Chalmers watched Livia, her black hair wet and lying close against her head so she looked almost otter-like. She turned her head and smiled at him. She was fine. He took the canoe back out into the center of the pool with a few quick strokes. She stood at the top of the bank and looked at the slide.

An otter popped its head out of the water not twenty feet from the boat and looked at Livia. Chalmers was surprised. The otters were very shy. The Dobines trapped them for their fur.

Livia spoke to the otter in Romanian. It dived, leaving a swirl on the surface of the pool.

"Watch me," Livia called.

She went down the slide feet first, hitting the pool with a splash. She stayed down a long time. Chalmers looked into the dark water. He was about to go over the side when she came up next to the canoe and grabbed the gunwale.

"I swim with them," she said.

Two otters surfaced only a few feet away from the canoe. They looked at him. Livia was on the other side.

She dived and disappeared. Chalmers looked down at the water but could see nothing. The otters surfaced first, near the bank, and then close to Livia. She continued to speak to them in Romanian.

The otters came out of the water and ran up the bank, their wet fur glistening in the sunlight. Livia stayed in the pool, treading water. Chalmers could not believe what he was seeing. In all the time he'd been on the river, he'd never seen the otters for more than a few seconds.

First one otter went down the slide and then another. They swam in circles around Livia.

"Swim with us," Livia urged.

But Chalmers couldn't make himself get out of the boat. He feared that his entering the water would break the spell.

"We have the same in Romania," Livia said.

She repeated the Romanian word.

"Lutra."

"Otter," he said.

"Otter," she said. "Otter, otter."

Livia climbed the bank with the animals and took her turn on the slide. Over and over they came down the slide. Livia began to do it like them, headfirst, her arms held along her sides.

She felt giddy. Once an otter had come close enough for her to touch, but she resisted the impulse to reach out and stroke its fur. As she went down the slide, she imagined her body suddenly changing before Chalmers' eyes, fur sprouting from her skin and webs growing between her fingers and toes. And Chalmers would sit in the canoe and watch, astonished at the metamorphosis. She imagined the peace such a change would bring. She would eat and play and make love. There would be no past, no future. Nothing to forget.

Chalmers sat in the boat afraid to talk because he might break the bond she'd managed to form so easily and quickly between herself and the animals.

At last the otters tired of the game and swam off upstream, disappearing behind a boulder. Livia made a last trip down the slide. He braced the canoe with the paddle to allow her to get in.

"Why not you slide with us?" she asked.

"They wouldn't slide with me," he said.

She'd turned around in the bow seat and faced him. He looked up into the trees so he wouldn't stare at her.

"I make love to you soon, Chalmers," she said. "For me it is not time. The death of Michael is heavy with me."

And Chalmers imagined making love to her in the canoe while it drifted about the pool.

"You don't want to forget him?" he asked.

"Not a man so good," she said. "He becomes something else for me. I must wait. Then there is room for us."

Chalmers paddled them down to the river. Once the sun had dried her body she dressed. He wondered if somewhere on a midstream rock the otters were basking in the sun and grooming their fur. He was going to be patient; he'd wait until she was ready.

Scott Ely

CHAPTER EIGHT

Livia was excited about Sunday lunch at Grandmother Rosa's, but Chalmers was not looking forward to sitting down to eat with Brother Sprott. It was going to be hard to contain his dislike for the preacher, the man who'd refused to say the words over his father or let him be buried at the church.

Chalmers put on a coat and tie for lunch. Grandmother Rosa set a formal table. He had trouble with the tie but finally got it knotted properly. Livia came out of the van wearing a black dress and a necklace of light wood carved into the shapes of animals: elephants, lions, giraffes.

"Your grandmother likes?" Livia asked. "She will be astonished."

Chalmers laughed.

"Oh, you're going to make her astonished," he said. "And the preacher too."

"A priest?"

"Like no priest you've ever known."

When Chalmers had called to say they were coming, Grandmother Rosa had been pleased.

"What's her name again?" she'd asked.

"Livia Tarna Mare," he said.

"Such a pretty name. Mare was her husband's name?"

"No, hers."

They drove into Susan Moore. Chalmers had explained to her about John David on the way.

"He'll be up and down that tree," Chalmers said. "Don't pay him any mind."

"Free like a child," Livia said.

Chalmers recalled that Grandmother Rosa had once said something like that.

John David was up in the tree when they arrived, dressed in a coat and tie. He stood on one of the big lower limbs. The purple harness looked strange against his seersucker suit. Grandmother Rosa made no exceptions for her Sunday lunches.

"Hello," Livia called up to John David

John David ascended the tree, vanishing into the leaves.

"Ah!" Livia cried.

She clapped her hands.

John David walked out on the end of a limb. It swayed under his weight. He stared down at Livia.

"John David, you are the emperor of trees!" Livia shouted.

John David smiled and pulled on a rope, swooping upward into the very top of the tree. Livia laughed and clapped her hands.

"Bravo!" she cried.

They couldn't see him but watched the branches moving. Finally all was still. John David was up there somewhere watching them. Looking up made Chalmers' neck hurt.

"Careful," Chalmers said. "Don't get him stirred up. Grandmother Rosa'll be mad at you if John David acts up at lunch."

By the time Chalmers opened the front door, John David was standing in the hallway by the coat rack. The purple harness was gone. There was a tear in the left leg of his suit, and the material was crumpled at his groin from the pressure of the harness. Chalmers had never seen John David look at a woman before as he was now looking at Livia.

"At lunch you sit with me," Livia said.

John David smiled and for a moment Chalmers thought he was going to hear him speak again. But instead John David reached out and touched Livia's necklace.

"You wear it," she said.

She took it off and put it around his neck. John David crossed the hallway and went up the stairs.

"You'll have a hard time getting it back," Chalmers said. "He'll put it in the tree."

"It is not important," she said.

Chalmers wondered if John David would come to lunch wearing the necklace. But John David had such a regard for

Grandmother Rosa that Chalmers doubted he would. John David would be worried enough about the tear in his pants' leg and the crumpled places on the suit.

They found Brother Sprott in the kitchen with Grandmother Rosa. She was frying chicken in an iron skillet. Chalmers smelled the corn bread and beans. He made his introductions.

"Our visitor from Romania," Brother Sprott said.

"I am American now," Livia said.

"Chalmers, you take Brother Sprott and Livia out on the porch," Grandmother Rosa said.

Chalmers thought Brother Sprott was grateful for the presence of Livia. He went on and on about the money he was raising to build a new and bigger church.

"That John David, he's a strange one," Brother Sprott said.

"The emperor of the trees," Livia said.

"The Lord is the only emperor," Brother Sprott said.

Livia smiled at him.

John David came onto the porch. He was wearing the necklace. Brother Sprott looked first at the necklace and than at Livia.

"You could carve an angel," he said.

"I make one with enormous wings," Livia said. "Like a butterfly."

John David smiled.

Brother Sprott looked at Livia suspiciously.

"You could make a beautiful angel," Brother Sprott said. "But you wouldn't. You'd make something else."

"Oh, no," Livia said. "It would be beautiful."

"Nothing I've seen of yours is beautiful," Brother Sprott said.

Chalmers wondered if Brother Sprott had paid a visit to Plumb's Bluff. He imagined that Livia would have told him about it if he had.

There was a silence. Livia smoothed out the material of her dress, bringing both her palms downward across her thighs. Brother Sprott took a drink of iced tea and looked out across the yard.

"We'll go help Grandmother," Chalmers said.

"No, let me," Brother Sprott said.

He got up and made his escape.

"Angels?" Livia said.

She laughed and Chalmers with her.

He wondered what kind of angel Livia might make. Maybe an angel with fangs and claws.

Grandmother Rosa appeared on the porch.

"Go find John David and tell him lunch is ready," she said.

They found John David hiding behind the oak. He was still wearing the necklace.

"You better not wear that to her table," Chalmers said.

John David shook his head and smiled.

Livia went up to John David and removed the necklace. She handed it to him and turned her back. He put it around her neck and fastened the clasp.

"What do you see from the treetops, John David?" Livia asked.

John David straightened his tie. He smiled again at Livia. Then he walked off towards the house.

"He lives all his life in the tree?" Livia asked.

"As long as I can remember," Chalmers said.

John David sat on one side of Livia and Chalmers on the other. Brother Sprott asked the blessing. Chalmers was grateful that Livia bowed her head.

"Miss Tara Mare, I want you to come to our church next Sunday," Grandmother Rosa said.

Brother Sprott was working on a drumstick and just nodded. Chalmers didn't think Brother Sprott looked pleased at the thought of Livia in his church. The preacher washed the chicken down with sweet tea.

"Miss Tara Mare, what are those things you make?" he asked.

"My sculptures?" Livia asked.

"They aren't real," Brother Sprott said.

"Macon," Grandmother Rosa said.

"She's an artist," Chalmers said.

"An artist who makes monsters," Brother Sprott said.

Brother Sprott stood up.

"I can no longer baptize those who've come to Jesus because of her," Brother Sprott said. "She swims naked at the Nectar Bridge. She has polluted the Nectar Pool."

Chalmers looked at Livia.

Chalmers imagined Brother Sprott standing hidden by the

cane on one of the banks and watching Livia swim in the pool. He wondered why Livia had returned to the pool and what she thought as she swam there. Chalmers thought of Suzannah's bath in the Bible. He wondered if Brother Sprott thought of that while he watched her swimming and what had stirred in him besides his outrage at her supposed desecration of the baptismal pool.

"While your creatures watched," Brother Sprott added.

Brother Sprott stood up. Grandmother Rosa tugged at his sleeve, but he refused to sit down. Livia was laughing. John David grinned foolishly.

"They are sculptures," Livia said.

Livia hadn't know exactly why she'd returned to the pool or why she'd set up the bird man and insect woman on the river-bank. She photographed them standing amid the tangle of vines on the bank and on the gravel bar where Chalmers had pulled her out of the water.

Then she'd swum in the pool for a long time. The water was considerably warmer than the day she'd stepped off the bridge with marble around her neck. She'd dived down to the bottom of the pool and had run her hands over the sand and mud, searching for the marks her feet or the marble might have made. But she could find nothing. The currents had swept it clean.

She floated on her back in the pool for a long time, looking up at the trees and masses of grapevines, listening to the bird songs. And she realized that she'd come not to remember but to erase the memory of that day. Now it had become just another pool on the river. She'd smiled at the thought of that, relaxing her body further, letting a gentle current take her so that the tree-tops and the blue sky turned slowly above.

And all the while Brother Sprott had been watching her. She wished that he'd made himself known. Then they could have talked, and he'd have lost his fear of her.

"Sit down, Macon," Grandmother Rosa said.

She stood up and tried to push him down into his chair.

"Devils!" Brother Sprott shouted. "Abominations in the sight of God!"

"Go home, Macon!" Grandmother Rosa said. "Go home!"

Brother Sprott was up again. Livia had her hand over her mouth, overcome with laughter. Chalmers was caught between laughter and anger.

"Chalmers, you lie with her and you lie with the Devil," Brother Sprott said.

John D

avid began to laugh. Grandmother Rosa put her hand on his arm, and he stopped.

"You can not speak like that at my table," Grandmother Rosa said. "Go home, Macon!"

Chalmers could tell she was really angry now. Brother Sprott knew it too.

"Good afternoon," Brother Sprott said.

He went out of the room.

"I want to apologize for him," Grandmother Rosa said to Livia. "So much has gone on with this family that it confuses him. I'm sure you'll have an apology."

Livia was still laughing, and Chalmers joined her. Then Grandmother Rosa began to laugh too.

"He's always been so pompous," Grandmother Rosa said. "But he can do good things."

"Like not let Daddy in the graveyard," Chalmers said.

"Hush," Grandmother Rosa said. "Randall is where he'd like to be."

Livia put her hand on his arm. Chalmers told himself that arguing with Grandmother Rosa would serve no purpose.

"Now tell us about Romania," Grandmother Rosa said to Livia.

Livia told the story of what had happened to her family. And how she'd met Michael in France.

"Just think," Grandmother Rosa said to Chalmers. "You sell me that land, and you and Livia could go to France."

Chalmers had to admire Grandmother Rosa. She never gave up. She'd turned the outburst from Brother Sprott into something to her advantage. She'd been the calm one, soothing the injured Livia. He wondered if she'd planned it all.

While Livia and Grandmother Rosa talked, Chalmers cleared the table and loaded the dishwasher. Livia was telling stories about Romania. John David had changed clothes and returned to the tree.

Grandmother Rosa came into the kitchen. Livia had gone out to watch John David.

"I like that girl. She has some sense."

"Brother Sprott doesn't think so," Chalmers said.

"Macon likes to hear himself talk," Grandmother Rosa said.

Chalmers poured himself a cup of coffee.

"I never liked him," Chalmers said.

"Would you rather Randall be at the church," she asked.

"No."

"Then leave it alone. You should be back in church. Or find another one. Take Livia with you."

"How about the Catholic Church?"

She laughed.

"I don't care. You need to belong to a church."

Chalmers promised he'd think about it. She talked about John David and the price of coal but never returned to the subject of buying his land as he expected she would.

Livia came in and they said goodbye. As they went out of the house and down the walk, John David lowered himself like a spider out of the oak. Livia walked over to him.

She held the necklace out to John David. She saw that Chalmers was watching them, but he was too far away to hear anything either one of them spoke.

"Take it," she said.

John David hesitated.

"You go on the river with him?" he asked.

"Sometimes," she said.

She pushed the necklace into his hands, and he took it.

"It is yours," she said.

"That river's a mean one," he said.

"I go with Chalmers," she said.

"I dream of that river."

"What kind of dreams?"

"Rushing water. Like out of a fire hose. Too fast to swim in. Current'll suck a person under. Lot's of people been drowned in that river."

"Do you drown in your dreams, John David?"

"I won't drown." He smiled. "I see the river from the bridge. When me and Miss Rosa go to Birmingham. I've never seen it up close. Don't want to."

"Chalmers will keep me safe."

"I suppose."

He turned and went up into the tree, his climbing irons making sharp clicks against the bark. She went to join Chalmers on the porch.

"What did he say?" Chalmers asked as they got in the truck. "He's never talked to me. I don't think he talks much to Grandmother."

"He speaks of his dreams," Livia said.

"Does he talk in sentences?"

"Yes."

She pointed at the tree. John David was in the topmost branches. He waved at them.

"What kind of dreams?" Chalmers asked.

"Of the river?" she said.

"What about the river?"

"He does not say precisely. He talks of the water. Of its power."

Chalmers imagined his grandmother telling John David about his father's death. It was no wonder that John David dreamed of the river.

"I dream about it too," he said.

"And yours?" she asked.

"I'm swimming toward my father. Underwater. I see things that live in the river: fish, turtles, otters. I see my father. He's smiling at me. Then I wake up. I never reach him."

She put her arms around him and laid her head against his chest.

"It is a good dream of your father," she said.

Livia did not want to speak to Chalmers of forgetting. She thought it best to let part of him live in the dream. She had no dreams of her family. All her sleep was a gray blankness. She did not think she wanted to dream of them.

"Let us go back to Plumb's Bluff," she said.

A few pieces of bark fell down around them. Chalmers looked up and saw John David, a smile on his face. He thought how sometime he might ask John David to tell his dream, to see if his was the same.

"Goodbye, John David," Livia called. "Goodbye."

She took his hand, and they went down the walk.

They left Susan Moore and started back to the river. Livia put her hand on his shoulder as he drove. Chalmers imagined she was measuring him for a piece of sculpture, feeling the muscle and bone beneath his skin so she'd know how to carve the stone in a manner that would make it appear to be living flesh, the reality Brother Sprott demanded.

CHAPTER NINE

The moon was well above the ridge, its light softening the outlines of the rocks and making the foam and froth appear even whiter. Chalmers sat in an eddy, his back toward Plumb's Run, the pistol in the box lashed to a thwart. He was paddling a plastic canoe, not a race boat. The plastic canoe was practically indestructible and would permit him to make mistakes. It also had a larger volume than a race boat, allowing him to better deal with the big waves and deep holes that were waiting for him. He wore a wet suit and a kayaker's helmet. On his life vest he'd strapped a skin diver's knife in case the boat got pinned against a rock with him inside it and he had to cut himself out. A carabineer was attached to the other shoulder of the jacket, but there would be no one there to put a rope on it and pull him out of the river, at least not while he was alive.

He went over the moves he'd have to make to get through the rapid safely. Running it alone, with no one to help if he got in trouble, always made him afraid. No matter how many times he did it, he found himself lingering in the eddy as if he were waiting for a starter's signal.

He knew that eventually he'd turn out of the eddy and go down into Plumb's Run. He'd sit in the eddy behind the big rock, at the center of the S, waiting for a canoe to come into the eddy. They wouldn't be able to see him until it was too late. If they were carrying wire, he'd deal with them right there, out in the middle of the river.

Livia had complained about his hunt for the killers, but Chalmers couldn't bring himself to stop.

Scott Ely

"You must promise me," she'd said.

"Won't be able to keep it," he'd said.

"Why?"

"They killed my daddy. I took him off the wire."

"You must forget."

"Can't."

Then she'd kissed him on the cheek and left him alone.

"It makes me sad, Chalmers," she'd said.

This night she was away, gone to Birmingham. She was having dinner with a woman who owned a gallery.

He spun the boat out of the eddy and entered the rapid. He went over the first five-foot drop, leaning downstream when the boat hit the bottom and catching it on a low paddle brace, the paddle acting like an outrigger. He made a ferry to avoid a mid-stream rock. Then he caught the eddy on the left side of the river. He sat in the eddy, the boat rocked by the turbulence. He felt himself trembling. He put the paddle over his head and stretched to loosen a tight muscle in his upper back. He took a number of deep slow breaths, sucked in great mouthfuls, of the mist-charged air. Ordinarily, on any other river, he'd have felt exhilaration, but instead there was only the dull, heavy sensation of fear. It was as if his veins were filled with sand.

Directly downstream from the eddy, that safe place where he rested, was a collection of undercut rocks. The current boomed against them, throwing up spray, shining white in the moonlight. When he turned out of the eddy, he'd have to ferry across to the right side of the river, not allowing the powerful current to sweep him into the rocks. To do it he had to get the angle just right so the current would push him across instead of sweeping him downstream.

He took a final deep breath and drove the canoe out of the eddy. He leaned hard downstream, so the current wouldn't catch a gunwale, and the boat shot across the river. He reached the right side of the river, paused in the eddy, and then turned the boat and paddled it hard to the center. The second two-foot drop was easy, but he had to guard against taking on water from the big standing wave that marked a hole, a place where the river went over an underwater rock, because he immediately had to make an eddy behind a rock to his right. More undercut rocks were waiting downstream.

He ran the drop. As he came over it he turned the boat across the top of the wave, which loomed much higher than his head. The canoe rose up, he dug the paddle hard against the downstream side, and the boat turned parallel to the current and shot into the eddy. He dug the paddle into the water, letting the boat spin around it. He sat facing upstream, his head turned downstream as he searched the river for wire.

He ferried to the left side of the river and ran the third drop on the left hand side, taking refuge in an eddy behind a boulder. Twenty yards away was a collection of car-sized boulders. The current boiled as it came against them, running through here and there in places where no boat could go. He ferried the boat across to the right hand side of the river and went downstream, catching an eddy behind a boulder.

Below, the river necked down to a place that was not much wider than the length of a canoe, forming a chute. Below the chute was a hole with a big standing wave. This was the place in the rapid where he'd string a wire if he wanted to kill someone. It would be a simple matter for one man to toss a rope across and another to pull the wire over. It could be anchored to a big pine on one side and a lighting-scarred poplar on the other. The wire would rest at the base of the wave, hidden in the foam. It would be certain death.

He went down the chute and into the eddy behind the huge boulder. He paddled the canoe to the upper end of the eddy where there was a crack in the largest boulder. If they came by canoe, he'd be waiting in the eddy for them; or he'd see them when they stepped out in the moonlight onto that bare rock if they came down from one of the ridges.

From the ammo box he took the pistol and hung it over a thwart. He unfastened the thigh straps and sat on the top of the pedestal seat. He waited. He let his mind float free and tried not to think of the passage of time. He worked hard at thinking of nothing, imagining a sort of gray blankness as if he were staring at the side of one of the big boulders. He especially tried not to think of Livia. That was how he passed the night. When he looked at his watch for the first time, it was a little after midnight.

He'd calculated that the stringing would most likely be done before midnight. That would give them time to reach the Nectar Bridge, which was at least two hours away, unload the canoe, and be home before daylight. Or if they came by foot it would give them time to climb out of the gorge.

He returned the pistol to the box and seated himself on the pedestal seat, pulling the straps tight over his thighs. Then he carefully worked his way down through the bottom half of the S, catching every eddy he could and checking for wire ahead at the most likely spots. They could conceal it in the water, but it would have to be anchored somewhere. So he looked for those places.

Then he reached the place where the wire had caught his father. For some reason he couldn't explain, he always ran that section blind. No scouting.

After he was past that, the rest of the run was easy. Here was a series of drops that could only be run on the left hand side. At the end was a ten-foot waterfall, but that was easy to run, as long as he got his line right when he went over it and avoided a rock at the bottom. It was the maneuvers above that were difficult. He had to be careful, for there were plenty of good places to string wire, since the only possible path lay through narrow chutes over the drops.

He was relieved when he brought the boat to rest in an eddy at the foot of the rapid. Yet at the same time he felt, as always, disappointment. If he'd caught someone stringing wire, there'd have been an end to things.

A river birch overhung the eddy, creating a denser patch of darkness. Breathing hard, he popped the Velcro-fastened thigh strips off his legs and sat up on the pedestal seat. He massaged his sore left knee. When he glanced toward the bank, he saw he wasn't alone. There was a square-ended john-boat in the eddy.

"I didn't do nothing."

The disembodied voice, with its sharp edge, came out of the darkness.

Pick Dobine squatted in his hill man's manner amidships.

"No one said you did," Chalmers said.

Chalmers wondered what he'd do if he discovered a coil of wire in the boat.

"Them folks from Birmingham cut my lines," Pick said. "But I never strung no wire."

Pick turned on an electric lantern. He played the light over his boat. There were coils of trotlines, a net, a red cooler. And four or five cooters in a wire basket. The turtles withdrew their heads into their shells when the light fell on them.

"I've been checking my traps," Pick said.

Pick's narrow face was illuminated by the lantern. He looked at the ammo box in Chalmer's boat.

"I knowed you been carrying that pistol," Pick said. "Most everybody knows."

"Who do you think did it?" Chalmers asked.

"No Dobine," Pick said quickly.

Chalmers laughed.

"But maybe a Price or a Luckett?" Chalmers said.

They were the other families who fished and trapped on the river.

"I don't know about them boys," Pick said. "All I know is about my own."

"You tell me what you know," Chalmers said.

Pick switched off the lantern.

"That sculptor girl's a strange one," Pick said.

"How's she strange?"

"Swims with no clothes on in the Nectar Pool. Folks get baptized in that pool. Brother Reese baptized me there."

"You saw her?"

"No, Brother Sprott. She puts devil statues out to watch."

Chalmers considered explaining to Pick that Livia was an artist but realized he'd be wasting his time.

"You seem to know a lot," Chalmers said. "You sure you don't know who strung that wire?"

The current circulating in the eddy pulled him close to Pick's boat. The gunwales kissed. Chalmers pulled them apart with a single paddle stroke. He smelled the sweet scent of wintergreen from the tobacco Pick was chewing.

Pick spit his plug into the eddy.

"I done told you," Pick said. "I don't know. You keep tearing up and down this river with that pistol, you're gonna wind up shooting somebody. Could be you'll shoot somebody like me. Somebody that's just out here trying to make a living. You think about that."

Pick paused. "I wouldn't be surprised if Brother Sprott preached against her. What would you do about that? I guess you could shoot him."

"Only person I'll be shooting is the one I catch stringing wire," Chalmers said.

"I'll guess you'll do what you got to do," Pick said.

Chalmers wondered if it would be worth going to talk with Brother Sprott about Livia.

"Now if you'll excuse me, I got lines to tend," Pick said.

"You see anyone stringing wire, you let me know," Chalmers said.

Pick promised he would.

"You remember that anybody could've strung that wire," Pick said. "Not just river folks."

Pick started the motor and went out of the eddy, headed downstream. Chalmers thought he was going too fast but imagined that Pick had the location of all the rocks memorized.

Chalmers sat in the eddy, listening to the sound of the motor fade away. Then the sound of the motor was gone. He lingered in the eddy and thought about Livia. If she kept swimming at Nectar Pool, she was going to make it difficult for both of them to live in the county. But at least she wasn't jumping into the river with a block of marble tied around her neck.

He turned the boat out of the eddy, letting the current carry it downstream. The current quickly played out, and he paddled the canoe through the dark, the rocks appearing as shapeless dark lumps above the lighter plane of the water. He paddled toward Nectar Bridge, two hours away. There would be some minor shoals but no real rapids. Now he thought of nothing but Livia as he paddled home to her.

CHAPTER TEN

Chalmers woke late to a room filled with sunlight. There was the familiar throb of the air compressor along with the sound of Livia's chisel on marble. Today was Saturday. He'd planned to take a day off from training. He lay in bed and remembered his conversation with Pick the night before. How would the people in the county react when Brother Sprott preached against her?

Chalmers walked outside with a cup of coffee in his hand. He stopped in his tracks when he saw Livia at work on a large block of white marble, one of those he'd cut at the mine. The marble rested on wooden blocks. A block and tackle was tied around one end, the rope anchored overhead to a big poplar limb.

"Rudy Blount brought it here," Livia said.

Chalmers wondered how he'd slept through the arrival of the marble.

Livia was cutting away at one end. It was hard to tell what she was making.

"You're doing this for Rudy Blount?" Chalmers asked.

Chalmers imagined that Rudy had commissioned Livia to carve the block for him.

"No," Livia said.

"You bought this?" he asked.

"A gift."

"Gift?"

"Yes."

Livia ran her hand over the edge of the block.

"A fine white marble," she said. "Very good."

Chalmers couldn't imagine what had prompted Rudy Blount to have the marble delivered.

"You've got a commission from Rudy Blount?" he asked.

She shook her head and smiled.

"I work for you," she said.

He looked at the marble.

"I make a canoe," she said. "You go fast in it."

Chalmers had used a male mold before. Male molds were called plugs. After the boat was removed from the mold the layup would have to be sanded. It wouldn't come out silky smooth as was the case with a female mold. He was unsure of any problems that might arise from the use of a marble plug, but he could think of no reason why it wouldn't work.

"How will you make it?" he asked.

He knew Livia had a picture of the mold he was working on in her mind. She'd seen it often enough.

Livia showed him with her hands, pointing out where she'd remove marble. He'd have to watch her carefully to make sure she stayed within racing specifications. She was going to widen the boat in the bilges more than he'd planned and increase the tumblehome. Tumblehome was a bulge in the upper part of the sides that narrowed the width of the boat at the gunwales, allowing a paddler easier access to the water.

"You go fast," she said.

Chalmers considered that instead of working herself away from those toothed figures with sculptures of rattlesnakes, she was going to spend her energy on the plug. There'd be no guarantee that it would be a good boat. Instead there was every chance the design wouldn't work.

"Fast," she said.

She took his hand and placed it on the marble. She had no doubt that design would perform as she'd promised. When the marble had appeared, unasked for, it was a sign. Like the meeting on the train, like the truck not being searched. Like Michael in the cafe. She believed she intuited what design Chalmer's dead father had intended.

"You could make something else out of this," he said.

She could make otters or turtles or even a long-nosed gar, its mouth filled with needle sharp teeth. She was good at making teeth.

"A boat," she said. "For you."

He started to take his hand away, but she pressed it against the stone.

"It is inside," she said.

He looked at her dark eyes. He imagined her swimming in Nectar Pool.

"You believe I can carve it?" she asked.

Chalmers removed his hand from the marble.

"Yes," he said.

He felt that quietness again. He took her hand. Her fingers were rough from her work with the stone. He looked at the marble, at the pile of chips that had accumulated from her work.

"Who'd have thought there'd be marble on top of that coal," he said.

"Michael said it would be there," she said.

"He was thinking of Georgia," he said.

She laughed.

"It was there," she said.

She put her hand on his cheek, her palm slick with marble dust.

Now he was going to make a canoe around the plug she carved. If her design failed, he'd be forced to race an old boat. There might not be time to make another mold. He didn't think he wanted to work on his own design simultaneously. That wouldn't show much confidence in her. Besides he was stuck. He had no idea how to proceed.

"You go on the river to kill people," she said. "That pistol in the box. Why do you do that, Chalmers?"

"They killed my father," Chalmers said.

"And you kill them. Then you no longer are Chalmers Plumb. I know it happens. I know."

"I'll take them to the sheriff."

"No!"

She was crying now, the tears making tracks in the white dust.

"You will kill them!" she said. "You stop now! Promise me!"

Chalmers considered making the promise. But he knew he wouldn't be able to keep it. If he wasn't careful, he was going to destroy what was happening between them.

"I can't," he said.

She hesitated before she spoke.

"Just tell me before you go," she said. "You stop one time and then two. It will be easy."

Chalmers said he'd think about doing that. This seemed to satisfy her.

Livia tried not to let Chalmers see how upset she was. It was a roulette-like game he was playing. He could sit in the eddy in Plumb's Run for six-months or six years and nothing would happen. Or the very next time he went, even if he told himself it was the last time, would be when he would kill people or they would kill him. She resolved that she'd find a way to make him leave Plumb's Bluff, step out of the game forever.

"Now you watch me work," she said.

She put on her goggles and mask and took up the chisel. Chalmers retreated to the table. And as he sat there he watched the bow of the boat begin to emerge from the square block. Livia was swift and sure in her decisions. The ends of the boat were going to be raised. That was correct. He'd heard that the race designer was planning to drop the gates at the Nationals. That meant there'd be no gap between the poles and the river to slide the front portion of the bow and thus save time. Paddlers would have to set up for each gate in a classical manner. A premium would be placed on the ability to maneuver the canoe, and some of the emphasis on pure downriver speed would be removed. Raised ends would allow the boat to be turned easier.

He sat on the table and watched her work on into the morning. Soon she was completely covered with white dust. The marble canoe was no illusion; Livia was a real woman. If Pick Dobine was somewhere off in the trees watching, he'd have another strange story to tell. Chalmers imagined how the story would be altered and magnified. People would be talking about how Chalmers had taken a marble canoe down through the gates.

CHAPTER ELEVEN

Chalmers woke early on Sunday morning. He put on a white shirt, a tan suit of his father's—custom tailored from a leave in Hong Kong—a pair of shoes he'd bought in Birmingham, and one of his father's ties.

He went out of the trailer. Livia was still asleep in the van, the mosquito netting she'd draped over the open door hanging limp and shiny with dew in the absolute stillness of the early morning. He walked closer and listened to the sound of her steady breathing. She lay curled on her cot. The bird man and insect woman stood against the wall of the van. She'd destroyed the pair of snake sculptures, saying she'd made a mistake in attempting them. She still felt the need to make more of the toothed cubes. Chalmers had noticed that every evening she packed everything away. It was as if she wanted to be able to drive off one morning without even a goodbye.

He drove slowly by the block of marble, the bow of the plug emerging from it as if it were something alive growing out of that dense white stone. Once he was well away from Livia's van, he drove fast on the gravel road, the brown dust boiling up in twin plumes behind him. He didn't want to be late for church. This was the Sunday Brother Sprott was going to preach against Livia.

The churchyard was filled with cars and trucks. Edward met him on the front steps.

"You said you'd never come back," Edward said.

"It's because Brother Sprott's got himself all worked up over Livia," Chalmers said.

"Folks are talking bad about that woman," Edward said.

Chalmers saw people he'd known all his life. Friends of his father and grandfather and girls he'd dated. Some of the older men wore the same suits that Chalmers had seen them come to church in when he was a boy. The younger people were dressed in the latest fashions. The girls walked unsteadily in their new heels. The boys had washed off the grime of farm and mill and knotted ties around their necks. Chalmers wondered if he looked as awkward as they did. Some spoke; most didn't. A girl he'd dated smiled at him but then lowered her eyes at a word from her mother.

"Miss Rosa don't want him to do it," Edward said. "He wouldn't listen to her."

"He can say what he wants," Chalmers said. "But I'm talking too."

They went into the church. The simple wooden benches were arranged in rows. A few metal folding chairs were set up. It looked like Brother Sprott was expecting a big crowd. The place always smelled of pine from where the carpenter bees had bored holes in the exposed rafters. Once John David had gotten restless and climbed up into those rafters.

Grandmother Rosa was sitting in her usual place in the first row. She stared straight ahead. John David had turned around, a big grin on his face. His tie was crooked.

Chalmers sat down next to John David. Grandmother Rosa looked at him for the first time.

"You let Brother Sprott have his say," she said. "Then you can talk. I'll talk too."

Edward's mother played the electric organ, and led by Brother Sprott they sang hymns. Chalmers caught Brother Sprott's eye from time to time. The preacher was clearly uncomfortable, and Chalmers hoped that just his presence would be enough. Brother Sprott could fall back onto one of his usual performances. He'd talk about their sins and describe the torments of Hell that were awaiting them. Unless they let Jesus save them. Brother Sprott was a good speaker. He'd start off calm, but before a sermon was over, he'd be sweating, even if it was January, and the congregation would be yelling and screaming. Grandmother Rosa had been caught up in it. So had Chalmers.

Then the time for the sermon came. Brother Sprott turned and looked directly at Chalmers.

"I see that Chalmers Plumb is with us," Brother Sprott said.

Chalmers heard the murmur of the congregation.

"He's come back to the Lord," Brother Sprott said. He paused and looked out over the congregation. "Before it's too late."

John David was grinning. But this was normal behavior for him.

"The Sierra Club has been talking about buying the river," Brother Sprott said. "They'll put up a sign saying who owns it. That sign'll say that the people of Alabama or maybe even the people of these whole United States own it. Fools. That's like those folks from Birmingham and Atlanta. Laying claim to what belongs to Him."

"That's right, brother," a woman cried.

"Praise the Lord!" a man shouted.

"God will look down on those fools," Brother Sprott said. He paused. "Maybe the Lord'll just laugh. Sit up there and look at those fools and their sign and laugh."

"He's the boss!" another man shouted.

Brother Sprott looked out over the congregation. No one else spoke. They were all waiting for him. The scent of perfume drifted over Chalmers' bench.

"Now someone has come among us from far away," Brother Sprott said. "From a distant land. Chalmers Plumb is here because he knows what she is. Beware of that woman!"

"You go on outside, John David," Grandmother Rosa whispered. "Go climb."

John David got up and slipped away down the aisle. Once John David had made animal-like sounds during a sermon. Then he'd climbed up into the rafters and began to jabber. They'd had considerable difficulty getting him down. Brother Sprott had claimed the Lord was talking through him. That was the last time Grandmother Rosa had allowed John David to sit through a sermon.

"Swimming before her devils is what she does," Brother Sprott said. "Swimming naked."

"Save her, Jesus!" a woman shouted.

"He'll save her if she asks," Brother Sprott said.

He raised his arms above his head.

"The Lord can do anything," he said. "Love anyone. No matter how black with sin."

Scott Ely

"Praise the Lord!" a second woman shouted.

Brother Sprott shook his head in agreement and held up his hands, palms facing out, for silence.

"She makes statues of devils." He paused. "I've never seen anything like 'em. How does she know what they look like?" Again he paused. "She's looked into the face of the Devil. That's how. She swims naked under their eyes in the Nectar Pool. Where we bring men and women and little children to Jesus."

"Oh, Jesus!" a woman's voice moaned.

"That's right, sister," Brother Sprott said. "Jesus would help her if she asks. But the Devil is at her ear. Whispering to her. Making her think unnatural thoughts, perform unnatural acts. Jesus could save her."

Chalmers stood up.

"Sit down Chalmers," Grandmother Rosa urged. "Sit down."

"You seen her do it?" Chalmers asked. "Watched her swimming naked? That doesn't seem to me to be something a preacher should be doing."

Brother Sprott looked out over the congregation. People began to talk to each other.

"Yes, I've seen," Brother Sprott said. "It is my duty to look. It is my duty to warn everyone of her. She is an abomination in the sight of the Lord."

"Save us, Jesus!" a man cried.

"The devil must be rooted out of that woman," Brother Sprott shouted.

More people from the congregation cried out.

"Stop it!" Chalmers shouted. "Stop it!"

He stood up on the bench and turned to the congregation. Grandmother Rosa pulled at his pants' leg.

"Sit down, Chalmers," she said.

"They're just statues," Chalmers said.

"Images of what she has seen," Brother Sprott said. "Creatures of darkness. Creatures of sin."

"Devils!" a woman yelled.

"Git away from her, Chalmers!" another woman shouted.

"Chalmers is back in church," Brother Sprott said. "He's been born again. I baptized him in the Nectar Pool, the pool she's polluting. Jesus will save him."

People began to scream. A woman reached out and wrapped

her arms around Chalmers' legs.

"The lamb is in the fold again!" Brother Sprott shouted. "Save him Jesus!"

"Jesus! Jesus! Jesus!" a female voice began to chant.

"Go home, Chalmers," Grandmother Rosa said.

"Livia Tarna Mare," Chalmers shouted. "A woman. No devil."

"The devil is cunning," Brother Sprott shouted. "Listen to Jesus! Listen to Jesus!"

The congregation were out of their seats now, surging around him and Grandmother Rosa.

"Lay hands on him!" Brother Sprott shouted. "Let the holy spirit flow from you to him. The holy spirit has filled all of us."

People shrieked. They closed in and laid their hands on him. He smelled perfume and sweat and tobacco. He felt the caress of thin hands, of fleshy hands. He saw Edward sitting on a bench. Edward looked sad.

"Heal him!" Brother Sprott shouted. "Heal him!"

Chalmers broke free. A woman screamed. Voices called out to Jesus.

"Chalmers!" Grandmother Rosa cried.

He ran down the aisle, people's hands clutching at him, and then out the doors and into the bright sunlight. No one followed him. He turned his back on them and walked across the gravel lot to his truck.

"Jeeeeesus!" a shout came from the big poplar at the edge of the lot.

It was John David's climbing tree.

Chalmers looked up and saw John David in the top of the tree waving at him. Chalmers waved back.

"Jeeeeesus!" John David shouted again.

He looked back to the doorway of the church and saw Brother Sprott standing there looking at John David. John David gave his cry again. Brother Sprott shaded his eyes against the sun.

It was as if, Chalmers thought, John David was some well-dressed angel who'd floated down from heaven to perch in the top of the tree.

"John David, come down from there," Grandmother Rosa demanded.

John David waved to her.

Chalmers caught Grandmother Rosa's eye. She looked unhappy, her shoulders sagging slightly in a way he'd never seen before. He would go see Grandmother Rosa later in the week. He thought she liked Livia. Grandmother Rosa could speak again with Brother Sprott; maybe she could persuade him to stop preaching against Livia.

As Chalmers drove out of the lot, John David was descending, a figure in blue and white seersucker coming down through the green leaves, while at the foot of the tree Brother Sprott and Grandmother Rosa, along with the congregation, waited to receive him.

CHAPTER TWELVE

Chalmers found Livia at the picnic table when he returned from the church. She had a camera set up on a tripod and was taking pictures of the statues. The bird man stood beside the insect woman. Livia had arranged pieces of her sculpture on the table.

"Pictures for galleries," Livia said. "For my friend in Birmingham."

She looked through the camera at the scene she'd composed.

"Move Ivan," Livia said.

Chalmers hadn't known she'd given names to the statues. He picked up Ivan. The statue was surprisingly light. The large black and brownish feathers had a musty smell to them. They could be the feathers of a crow or a turkey vulture. Or maybe not that at all. The feathers might be from some bird native only to Eastern Europe. If it suddenly appeared in the river trees, it would drive the Alabama birds into a frenzy.

"To the right," Livia said.

She was crouched behind the camera. He moved Ivan about until she was satisfied. Then he stepped away from the table. She shot up a roll of film.

"Ivan?" he asked.

She laughed.

"Michael gives them names," she said. "The woman is Phoebe."

She altered the composition again and had him move Phoebe about until she was satisfied. Phoebe was much heavier than Ivan.

Her insect's thorax was made of wood. He ran his hand over its shiny smooth surface.

"African wood," she said. "Very dense, very heavy. Difficult to carve."

"You're going to sell them?" he asked.

"Perhaps," she said.

He wondered if he should tell her about what happened at church. But he realized that it would be difficult to make her understand. It was good she was thinking of visiting galleries. That would get her out of the county for a time.

"I want to make pictures on the river," she said.

Chalmers considered the events at the church. He decided he didn't care. Maybe it would be a good thing if she was seen with him on the river. Some people would understand she was simply an artist.

He agreed. They loaded the canoe onto the truck along with the pieces of the sculpture and Ivan and Phoebe. She explained she wanted to find a shallow place in the river. He thought that Three Mile Shoals would be a good choice. This time of year there was barely enough water to float a canoe.

She frowned when he put the ammo box in the boat and lashed it to a thwart. He'd parked the truck at the edge of a gently sloping bank.

"For snakes," he said.

"Yes, it will be good for snakes," she said. "What kind?"

"Cottonmouths," he said.

He expected she was going to ask him what a cottonmouth looked like, but she said nothing.

They went down the river, through four small rapids, and reached Three-Mile Shoals. Here the river widened, the flow breaking up into dozens of channels. Herons stood motionless as they stalked fish. In the shallows, river grass and spider lilies grew. The heavy lily heads bobbed to the pulse of the current.

He worked the canoe down through the shoals. Sometimes they rode; sometimes it was necessary to get out and walk and tow the boat.

Midway through the shoals was a small island. On one side the water went down fast through a narrow chute; on the other the water cascaded over a series of one-foot drops, slabs of rock that extended all the way across the river. Huge poplars and oaks grew on the banks. A big white heron flew off at their approach.

"Here," Livia said.

He took the canoe over a small drop. They unloaded the statues and the marble sculptures in the pool below. Livia set up her camera. Chalmers wasn't sure if she was going to show the pictures she was making to the gallery owner or if she was making photographs that were works of art in themselves.

All afternoon she made photographs. She shot the toothed figures amid spider lilies and on logs where sunning turtles dived off at their approach. And Ivan and Phoebe always were part of the composition. Chalmers got used to the weight of each of them. He learned exactly how to place them without their tipping over. Phoebe was inclined to do that. Once one of Ivan's feathers came off. Chalmers put it in his pocket for Livia to reattach later.

Then she was done. The sun was low over the big timber. She packed up the camera, and they loaded the sculptures into the boat. They had a two-mile paddle ahead of them to a bridge where, as was his custom, Chalmers had hidden a mountain bike in the trees. He'd use it to go back for the truck while Livia waited with the boat.

They sat together on a rock. At the foot of the island the white heron was fishing the shoals. Livia stood up.

She thought that this river was not like the one where she and her mother and her sister had swum and played with otters. It smelled different; no mountains rose in the distance. She wondered what life would be like for Chalmers if he left Plumb's Bluff. She thought he should sell the coal to his grandmother and leave. But she considered that he might one day stand in a river somewhere and have it feel as alien to him as this one now did to her.

To Chalmers the heron looked like it might take flight but then settled down to stalking fish again, its head inclined to one side and its left leg raised partly out of the water.

"What is this river to you?" she asked.

Chalmers looked upstream for a moment before he spoke.

"My life," he said.

"You could leave here?" she asked.

"Never."

He was smiling.

"Come, we look at your river," she said.

She was pulling off her clothes. Then the shorts and top were gone, and she stood before him, her breasts swaying in the late afternoon sunlight. She dived into the shallow pool and swam up to where the water dropped down over one of the slabs. She stayed under a long time. He watched her in the clear water, her body white against a dark slab of rock. She surfaced, the water dripping off her body.

"Come and see, Chalmers," she said.

He took off his clothes and joined her.

"See what?" he asked.

He didn't want to play games in the river with Livia. He wanted to make love to her. But instead of kissing her as he wished, taking those beautiful breasts in his hands, he did as she asked.

"Open your eyes," she said.

Together they went under, the water nowhere deeper than three or four feet. He heard the rush in his ears. She was swimming only a few feet away from him. He saw a crayfish go scuttling away backwards, a school of minnows, a soft-shell turtle, and then, as he swam against the current, Livia's leg brushing his, he saw a three-foot gar feeding in the current, surrounded by its young. As he peered through the slightly roiled water, and Livia turned and smiled at him, he turned to the flash of a minnow that swam close to his head. Out of air, he surfaced.

"You see?" Livia asked. "Like through the eye of a fish?"

"I saw," he said. "Beautiful."

"Yes, beautiful."

Redtails had moved up into the shoal to feed. They stood on their heads, their tails swaying elegantly above the water.

And there, surrounded by the school of fish, he lay with Livia on a sandbar, the water barely deep enough to cover her back. The wet hair between her legs glistened in the sunlight.

"I learn your river," she said.

She noticed he had the same expression on his face as when he'd walked out of the trailer that morning and discovered her carving a canoe out of marble.

"You look at me like you did the marble canoe," she said.

He laughed.

"You're prettier than any damn canoe," he said.

Chalmers wished he had the words back. He knew that wasn't the right thing to say to a woman.

"Prettier than the most beautiful thing you know," she said. "I like that."

She lay down on the sand.

"We will make love beside your river," she said.

Chalmers felt very calm. The sunlight seemed too brilliant, and he wished they'd chosen a spot beneath a tree, not out here exposed on this miniature island in the middle of the shoal. He turned his head away from her and watched the heron spear a fish.

"Chalmers," she said.

He stepped toward her. His shadow fell across her breasts.

"This is going to be your river too," he said.

And then he was in her arms. Her hands felt cool against his back; the sun was hot.

Behind him he heard the flap of wings as a heron took flight. Its shadow passed over them.

Then she pulled him to her. He buried his face against her neck. He heard her breathing; he heard the rush of water over a drop. But then he was able to move away from all of it and reach a place that was out of the sun, beyond the rush of the water. They lay side by side on the sand. He had thrown his arm across his eyes to shield them from the sun.

"Us, Chalmers," she said.

He rolled onto his side and looked at her. Sand and pieces of leaf were caught up in her hair. He wished he knew how to say "I love you" in Romanian. Instead he said it in English.

Livia smiled when he said it.

"Love is good," she said.

Chalmers didn't press her for more.

They sat on the rock, waiting for their skin to dry. Phoebe's feathers had gotten a little wet, and they had a new sort of smell to them. Like autumn leaves.

"You like them?" she asked.

"I don't know," he said. "I mean I've never seen anything like them."

"I think you do not like. But we are like them. Breaking apart. We, all of us, Romanian and Americans. We fall apart."

Chalmers thought that "fall apart" was a strange term. He wondered what word she was searching for.

"Think of how you feel when you see the otters," she said. "Think of that. Not falling apart."

"Everyone should get naked and look at otters?"

They both laughed.

"No," she said. "Everyone be human. Live inside the earth. Not outside."

Chalmers didn't understand. She saw it on his face.

"Not make ourselves monsters," she said. "If Phoebe and Ivan are alive they die. Deformed. All of us deformed inside."

Chalmers looked at Phoebe and Ivan, at Ivan's one red eye and one yellow eye. Phoebe's eyes were a washed-out blue.

"You see?" she asked.

He thought of his father caught on the wire and Brother Sprott's sermon and his own desire to take revenge on his father's killers. Livia might be right. But he wasn't sure her words would keep him off the river with the pistol.

"Yes," he said.

"Good," she said.

She stood up and walked across the river on one of the slabs, picking her way carefully over the algae-slick rocks. Then she started up the bank.

"Livia?" he called.

She turned and laughed at him.

He followed her across the river.

When he reached the top of the bank, he saw no sign of her.

"Livia?" he called.

His voice echoed off the trunks of the big trees.

Then he heard her moving off behind a patch of cane. She stepped out in the open for an instant, the sunlight falling on her breasts, and laughed at him. She ran.

He'd thought she'd be easy to find, but she wasn't. He tripped over vines. Once he found himself in the center of a patch of poison ivy. Her laughter echoed through the trees.

Then land rose as he followed the sound of her laughter. Now it was all pine, the needles a soft carpet under his feet. He stopped, breathing hard, listening for the sound of her laughter or her feet on the needles, but heard nothing.

"Livia," he called.

There was no reply. A breeze rusted the tops of the pines. Above his head a squirrel was stripping a green pine cone, the pieces falling in a gentle rain on the needles.

He moved uphill and made his way through a honeysuckle thicket. Once his father had wounded a deer in this patch of woods. But they lost the blood trail and never found it. In the spring Chalmers had come upon its bones, picked clean by scavengers.

Past the thicket was a clearing in a stand of especially large pines. He came around a tree and there she was sitting on the pine needles. She was crying.

"What's wrong?" he asked.

She wiped the tears out of her eyes.

"Sometimes I swim in the river in my country and then run in the forest," she said. "I run until my legs desert me."

"You were afraid of something?" he asked.

"No, I loved to run in the forest."

He laughed.

"You can't do that around here," he said. "You'll step on a snake."

"Everywhere there are snakes in this country," she said.

"That's right. That's exactly right."

They lay together on their backs. He took her hand in his. Chalmers gazed at patches of blue sky through the treetops. He smelled the sharp scent of pines.

By the time they returned to the river, it was growing dark. The heron was gone. Bats twisted overhead. As they walked the boat down through the shoals, startled fish fled at their approach. Insects were loud from the woods. They reached the end of the island. Chalmers paddled them down a channel, the river narrowing again, and toward the bridge. Livia sat still and straight in the bow seat. They did not talk.

At the bridge Chalmers tried to leave the pistol with Livia. It was not a good place for a woman to be alone at night. She had him return it to the ammo box.

"No killing," she said.

He considered taking her with him, but it was five miles back to where they'd left the truck.

"Don't get up on the bridge," he said. "Stay down here with the canoe. Nobody'll even know you're here."

He'd drawn the boat up on a sandbar next to the bridge. There was a good chance that no one would even come across while he was gone. Off in the woods a whippoorwill was calling.

Chalmers rode the bike as if he were running a race, arriving at his truck covered with sweat and his legs rubbery. He tossed the bike in the truck and started back. As he dropped down the hill to the bridge, he saw taillights. Livia was talking with someone.

Pick Dobine got out of the truck when Chalmers drove up. Pick had his canoe in the back. Chalmers thought of Pick loading a coil of wire into the bow, imagining the rasping sound the wire would make on the aluminum.

"I thought I'd sit with her," Pick said.

"He catches catfish," Livia said.

Pick spit tobacco off into the river. Chalmers caught that wintergreen scent.

"Thanks for looking out for her," Chalmers said.

"Girl don't need to be out here all alone," Pick said.

Livia laughed.

"It's true," Pick said. "Some mean ones on this river."

"I'll get the boat," Chalmers said.

"Let me help," Pick offered.

When they got to the river, Pick wouldn't touch the boat until Livia had taken Phoebe and Ivan out of it. The marble sculptures didn't bother him, but he wouldn't come near the statues.

"Give me the jumps," Pick said. "How can you stand living with them things?"

Livia laughed.

"Touch one," she said. "They are not hurting you."

"I'd just as soon pick up a cottonmouth," he said.

So Pick helped Livia with the marble while Chalmers carried the canoe. Pick never stopped talking while Chalmers tied it on the truck. He went on and on about a big catfish he'd caught the day before. He pointed out that once his father had caught one that weighed nearly a hundred pounds.

"I promised her I'd bring you some catfish," Pick said as Chalmers got in the truck. "That all right with you, Chalmers?"

Chalmers said it was.

"You see my truck, you'll know it's me bringing you fish," Pick said. "Don't want you to start shooting."

Chalmers said he'd be expecting to see Pick's truck one day soon.

They left Pick on the bridge and started home.

"Pick Dobine says you want to shoot him," Livia said.

Chalmers could tell that Livia was seriously concerned.

"I might if I thought he'd strung the wire," Chalmers said.

He wondered how Pick was going to report their meeting to Brother Sprott. His version would provide material for future sermons.

"He wants to be your friend," Livia said.

"Dobines don't have friends," Chalmers observed.

He tried to explain to Livia the kind of people the Dobines were but failed.

"They are just poor," Livia said.

"A Dobine probably sticks a knife in somebody or gets one stuck in him at least once a month. Trouble is what they are. Something happens and they're the first place the sheriff looks."

Chalmers doubted whether he'd show up with any catfish.

"You will not shoot him if he brings fish?" Livia asked.

"I'm not going shoot anybody," Chalmers said.

"Good," she said. "Good."

"How will you cook this catfish?" she asked.

"Fried, I suppose."

Livia was sitting close to him. They both smelled of the river, a mud and water and damp wood smell. She was sniffing at a spider lily she'd picked. It had no scent, but she kept trying, her nose buried in the fleshy blossom.

"It doesn't smell," he said.

She inclined her head to him, still sniffing at the lily.

"No?" she asked.

"No," he said.

She put the lily on the seat beside her.

A group of deer suddenly appeared in the headlights. They froze for a moment, the truck sliding a bit as Chalmers applied the brakes. Then they melted away, their white tails flashing in the dark.

"Lovely," Livia said.

"Yes," Chalmers said.

Chalmers considered what she'd said about "falling apart." He knew he was going to keep running the river with the pistol in the ammunition box. But now he might leave a wire stringer to the sheriff.

"Pick Dobine touches the river and all that is in it?" Livia asked.

"Mostly he kills things," he said.

"I think he loves what he kills."

Chalmers laughed.

"Maybe," he said. "Dobines aren't big on love."

Chalmers liked the strange way she had of talking about the river and Pick. He thought that Pick was just as grotesque as Phoebe or Ivan. But Livia was looking at him with different eyes.

"I stay in Blount Country," Livia said.

"I want you to stay," Chalmers said.

He couldn't leave; he didn't want her to leave.

They drove through the insect-loud countryside, the headlights cutting through the darkness, the gravel rattling against the tires. Chalmers imagined himself no longer paddling the river looking for the killers of his father. And Brother Sprott no longer preaching sermons against Livia. Chalmers pictured himself winning the Nationals. There'd be no more blasting. Livia would work marble into soft and lovely shapes, and he'd build canoes.

CHAPTER THIRTEEN

Livia received a commission from Rudy Blount to make decorations for his bridge. Chalmers could see she was happy for the work, because she couldn't figure out how to proceed with her work on the marble plug. The shape of the canoe was emerging, but he had seen her sit for hours and stare at the unfinished plug, unable to make a decision as to the shape of the next cut.

Rudy's cousin had come back from Europe with pictures of cathedrals. Rudy had been fascinated by gargoyles.

"They put devils on their churches," Rudy said. "I don't want devils on my bridge. I want steers."

Rudy had three blocks of the white marble, left over from the laying of the footers, delivered to the trailer. Livia estimated she could cut six steers' heads out of them. Rudy wanted one on each side of the bridge at the center, facing upstream and downstream, and double steer heads at the approaches. The bridge was almost finished when Livia began work. Rudy was in the process of laying the steel frame over the marble footers. He'd moved a light crane out from the mine to handle the steel.

Livia worked hard on the steers' heads. It was strange watching the heads emerge from the white marble instead of the toothed figures. Chalmers noticed that although she worked all day at the heads, she didn't work with the same intensity he'd observed when she brought one of the toothed figures out of the stone with her chisel. The heads were playful renderings of steers with soft flowing lines. Some had horns that looked more like vines. Two were laughing. She'd painted their horns and eyes in bright colors.

She installed them on the bridge, all finished now except for the cypress deck. Rudy had planned a party to celebrate the laying of the last plank. Chalmers learned from Edward that Rudy had invited Grandmother Rosa and John David.

The day of the celebration they drove to the bridge, the gravel road pitching steeply down a hill to the river. As they came out of the trees, the first things they saw were the twin laughing steer heads set on pedestals flanking the western approach to the bridge. John David was walking one of the steel beams. He saw them coming and waved. Then he lowered himself from the beam with a brightly colored climbing rope. As they passed, he descended below the level of the roadway, dropping down to the river.

Rudy himself drove the nails in the last plank while his friends watched. Chalmers thought he drove them well, not missing a single nail head or stopping to rest, the hammer coming down rhythmically and clean.

"No flood'll wash this one away," Rudy said.

Rudy had raised the level of the bridge by ten or twelve feet. But the new highway bridges over the river, those that floods never reached, were twenty or thirty feet higher.

"I took the hundred-year high water mark and got five feet above that," Rudy said. "And this little lady made me steer heads. Ain't it the prettiest bridge you ever seen?"

Rudy gave Livia a hug and a kiss.

"Let's go dance and eat," Rudy said.

For two days Rudy had been barbecuing an entire steer in a pit over hickory coals. Blue smoke rose from the pit where the steer was cooking; tables were set up beneath the big oaks on a park-like stretch of ground. Rudy had fenced the cows out of it for the party. The grass had been cropped short by the cattle. Here and there were a few thistles, covered with purple flowers, that the cows had left alone.

A country band began to play. Rudy and Grandmother Rosa were the first to start dancing. Chalmers danced with Livia. A few people stared at Livia, but Chalmers was pleased that on this day at least Livia had been accepted as a member of the community. Then the dance was over and Chalmers poured himself and Livia a beer from one of the kegs. Rudy didn't go to church often. Many of his friends were just like him, and that was probably why no one cared about Livia. They hadn't been in church to listen to

Brother Sprott's sermons.

"Dance with me?" Grandmother Rosa asked Chalmers.

Chalmers took his grandmother in his arms. The band was now playing a slow sad song.

"All week Rudy sent me flowers," she said. "So I came."

"That's good," Chalmers said.

He glanced up on the ridge where Rudy intended to build a house one day. He might start this year if the bridge survived the winter floods.

Livia was dancing with Rudy. Livia looked over and smiled at them.

"Rudy is a good dancer," Grandmother Rosa said.

Chalmers hadn't seen his grandmother since that day in church.

"I had a long talk with Macon," she said. "He's sorry for what happened."

"I know what he's been saying about Livia," Chalmers said.

"Macon can be a good man," she said. "I remember when he started the church. The old one burned. Brother Wilson retired. And they sent us Macon. He raised the money and worked every day during the week on the building. The men came out to help on Saturday."

Chalmers tried to imagine Macon Sprott up on the roof of the church setting the rafters. Or laying concrete blocks, a level in his hand.

"He visited your grandfather when he was sick," she said. "Macon is good with sick people. It's hard watching people die. You do it sometime. You'll see. He makes it easier for them."

Chalmers had never watched anyone die. He thought of his father, thankful that he hadn't been there when Randall Plumb was caught on the wire. There would have been nothing Chalmers could have done. He'd have had to sit in his boat and watch helplessly as his father drowned.

"Macon was the son of a coal miner," she said. "His father died of the black lung when he was just a boy. He helped his mother raise his younger brothers. He educated himself. Worked his way through seminary."

"Should I bring Livia to church?" he asked.

His grandmother laughed.

"No, Macon isn't ready for that girl in church," she said. "But

I think it's all about died down. Folks got tired of hearing about her swimming in Nectar Pool. He'll baptize somebody there one of these days soon. That'll be an end to it."

Chalmers wondered if she really believed that. He didn't, but he said nothing.

Although Chalmers kept waiting for her to bring up the land, she never did. She felt light and brittle in his arms, with flower-like scent on her, a flower he'd smelled before somewhere but couldn't identify.

"Rudy wants to marry me," she said.

All Chalmers could see was the linking of two strip-mining companies. They'd own just about everything in four counties. For some reason the image of the land undulating as the charges went off came into his mind.

"I thought you were mad at him," Chalmers said.

"I can't stay mad at Rudy," she said.

Chalmers thought he didn't understand his grandmother at all. She and his father fought over the coal and that poisoned everything for them. Now she and Rudy had fought over land and suddenly she was willing to make up with him. It didn't make any sense.

"You stayed mad at Daddy," Chalmers said.

"You father was a stubborn man," she said.

The song was coming to a close. Rudy was whirling Livia across the ground. She was laughing at something he'd said.

"I'm not selling," he said. "To you or Rudy or both of you at the same time."

"I haven't asked you to sell," she said softly. "At least not today. Why shouldn't I want that land. And like I said before. You could take the money and carry that girl to France. Take her someplace where she won't stir people up."

Chalmers was sorry for what he'd said.

"You marry Rudy," Chalmers said. "He's a good man. I'm going win the Nationals this year and we'll live at Plumb's Bluff. On *my* land."

"Then you talk to that girl," she said. "She has to be careful how she acts around here. Tell her to stay away from the Nectar Bridge."

"I already have."

"Good."

The music ended.

"You going let me come to the wedding?" Chalmers asked.

"Both of you," she said.

Rudy announced it was time to eat. Chalmers and Livia sat on the tailgate of Chalmers' pickup under the shade of an oak and ate barbecue and baked beans and drank beer. Off to the north a big thunderhead was building up, the white puffy cloud, its edges trimmed with gray, towering higher and higher. The faint sound of thunder was in the distance.

"I've been trying to raise corn all summer on thunder and lightning," a man beside them said.

The people around them laughed.

Every day clouds built up, but it always rained somewhere else. It was typical summer weather.

Chalmers watched John David travel on a Tyrolean traverse from the top of the oak to the bridge. Everyone else was watching too. It took him a long time to cross. He either wasn't in a hurry or he'd gotten a rope tangled. For a long time he just hung there halfway between the bridge and the tree. Then he started moving again. They cheered when he reached the bridge. John David stood on a narrow steel beam and waved to them.

John David then stood perfectly still and looked upstream. The thunderhead had turned black. Chalmers wondered if John David could see all the way to Clay's Falls, a six-foot drop where the river necked down into a very narrow channel between rock banks. It was a dangerous place to be in a boat at high water.

John David yelled something Chalmers couldn't understand. Grandmother Rosa walked toward the bridge. She shouted through her cupped hands at John David to come down. Everyone in the park-like grove of oaks now turned to see what was happening.

"Come down," Grandmother Rosa yelled.

John David shook his head and pointed upstream.

Livia left Chalmers' side and ran across the grass to join Grandmother Rosa.

"John David?" Livia yelled.

"Water!" John David shouted as he dropped to the roadway.

Then Chalmers heard a faint rumbling sound. In an instant he knew. It had rained hard upstream, and a dam had been formed at the narrows below the falls out of tree trunks wedged in the rocky passage. That was what John David had seen, the water building up behind the dam. Now it had broken. They had only a few seconds to leave the low ground and escape across the bridge.

"Flash flood!" Chalmers shouted

Everyone knew what that was. It had happened on the river before although Chalmers had never seen one.

Chalmers yelled at them to run for the high ground across the bridge.

They all ran. Grandmother Rosa tripped and fell. Livia snatched her to her feet, and taking her hand pulled her along after her. Rudy carried a small child.

Their feet made a pounding sound on the boards. Chalmers glanced down at the river, scarcely a foot deep, the current sliding slowly past the marble footers. The greenish water was clear. A bass was holding in an eddy behind a footer. The growl had increased in volume. He was reminded of an early morning freight passing by his grandmother's house.

Then they were on the gravel and running up the incline. The roar was now exactly like a train, one of those early morning freights that had terrorized him when he was a boy. Chalmers looked at the bridge and saw John David drop from a girder to the roadway. Beyond him Chalmers could see the vehicles and an abandoned electric organ and the blue smoke rising from the barbecue pit. Just beyond the pit, separated by a barbed wire fence, cattle grazed. A few had raised their heads to the sound.

"Run, John David!" Grandmother Rosa screamed.

They heard the roar, but because of the trees and the hill, they couldn't see the water coming. Below, the bridge and pasture lay frozen in pastoral simplicity. Chalmers thought it looked like a painting. Now the cattle were running with that awkward gait of animals bred for meat. If they were deer, they might have escaped. He imagined the deer, sleek gray shapes flowing effortlessly to the high ground. Livia had taken his hand; she was squeezing it hard.

Then the water was at the bridge, filling the riverbed and overflowing. A log pressed against the girders for a few seconds before it was catapulted straight up into the air, tumbling end over end. The bridge shuddered, the sound of the tearing girders and splintering wood lost beneath the roar of the water. It slowly tilted on its side and was gone.

Across the river the cars and pickups were swept against the fence where they were held for an instant by the wire. Then the wire snapped, the cars borne by the flood across the pasture. Now there were upside-down cars and pickups and carcasses of drowned cattle floating amid the oaks. A few steers had made it to safety on Rudy's flower-planted ridge where they stood and regarded the brown water flowing past, their heads held low to the ground. The bridge had been slammed into the far bank where it had become entangled with a mass of tree trunks and limbs.

They all looked at the water in silence. It had already begun to drop. A woman was crying softly. A child laughed.

"It's God's judgment!" a woman shouted.

Her cry was taken up by others.

Kent Hall, who had graduated two years before Chalmers, came walking up shouting that Livia was the devil. Kent was a distant cousin.

Chalmers waited until he got close enough and then hit him hard in the face with a straight left. Kent dropped to the ground, holding his broken nose with both hands. Livia cried out.

The crowd was silent. Chalmers looked into their faces and thought how difficult it was going to be for Livia to live at Plumb's Bluff. But he knew that he didn't want to see her leave, and he didn't want to leave. He saw himself becoming further and further removed from the web of kin. There'd be other fights and one day, maybe in the parking lot of the crossroad store, something much worse might happen. He resolved to make himself stop carrying a pistol in the truck. Nothing good was going to come out of doing that.

"Take her out of here," Grandmother Rosa said.

Chalmers took Livia's hand. She was shaking when he closed his hand around hers, but then she was still. They went up the road together.

"No one dies?" Livia asked.

She was crying.

"No," Chalmers said.

John David had followed them, the carabineers on his climbing harness jingling. Chalmers motioned for him to go back. His hand hurt from hitting Kent.

"We go to Mobile?" Livia asked.

Chalmers thought of living in her dead husband's house.

"It's my land," Chalmers said. "I can't train in Mobile. We're staying here."

They'd almost reached the highway. A truck went by, changing gears as it rounded a curve. They'd cut across John Green's pasture, cross three soybean fields, and be at his cousin Codman's house. He asked one of Cody's kids—he hadn't seen any of them at the barbecue—to drive them to Plumb's Bluff.

"I stay also," Livia said.

John David had crept up along the side of the road to within thirty yards of them. They both turned to look at him.

"With you," she said.

"Did you see them," he said. "What do you think those people are going to be talking about tonight? You. They think you're a witch. That flood proved it to them. Brother Sprott will stir 'em up."

"I am not afraid."

"We're not leaving. But we sure better be afraid."

John David had crept closer. Chalmers motioned for him to go back.

John David's carabineers jingled. Livia moved away and talked to him. She kept her voice low. Chalmers heard a murmuring sound but couldn't make out the words. Then she was back at his side. John David went running down the road, his feet raising little puffs of brown dust.

"He saved us all," Livia said.

"Grandmother might let him stay through the sermon next Sunday," Chalmers said. "Let him climb in the rafters. Maybe preach a sermon himself. Direct from God."

They both laughed.

Then he led her across John Green's pasture where cows lazily cropped grass and through a tree line and across the first soybean field. The beans were well up, almost knee high, the green field falling away in smooth swells down to the river. Although there were houses and trailers close by, they were hidden by the trees. Chalmers and Livia walked alone, as if they were traversing some endless, uninhabited green plain.

CHAPTER FOURTEEN

Sometimes, just before Chalmers went to sleep, he'd think of the pistol lying encased in the foam. And he'd think of the warnings he received from Livia and even Pick Dobine. He remembered the river man's voice, coming out of that darkness charged with mist, warning him that he was going to shoot an innocent man. But at the same time it was as if the pistol had its own song to sing, a persistent lilting whine that presented him with the image of his father dangling on the wire.

He trained and worked at the mine, trying not to think of the pistol and what he might find one night on the river. No one said a word to him about Livia or the flood. Rudy was already at work on a new bridge. This time he claimed he was going to build it ten feet higher. Chalmers knew people were talking about Livia. He could see it on the clerk's face when he went into the store at the Snead's Crossroads to buy groceries.

Livia went to Birmingham to visit her gallery. Just before dark she called to say she'd be home late. Soon the full moon would be rising. He took the ammo box out of the closet. He hadn't argued with himself about it. He'd just walked by the closet, and the next thing he knew he was stooping to pick up the ammo box, which for some reason felt too light to have the pistol in it. He'd resisted opening it to check until he was putting the box in the canoe. The pistol was there along with a box of ammunition. He'd imagined Livia tossing the pistol off the bluff into the river.

He turned out of the eddy above Plumb's Run and went over the first drop and into the familiar eddy on the left side of the river. He worked his way down the river in the moonlight. It turned out to be an easy run; he made no mistakes.

Finally he sat in the eddy behind the big boulder. The air felt good, filled with mist from the rapid, the pulse of the water making a soothing sound. There was the smell of rock and mud and the trees.

Chalmers remained in the eddy under early morning, listening hour after hour to the rush of the rapid. He saw nothing and finally gave up his vigil. He went down through the rapid and made the flat-water paddle to Nectar Bridge.

As he approached the bridge he saw a light on the bank. It was on for a second and then went off. He brought the canoe into the bank. The light didn't come on again.

He tied the stern painter to a limb. Then he carefully climbed out of the boat, lowering himself slowly into the water. He stood waist-deep in the river and listened for any sound from the bank. Anyone on the river at night was a suspect. But he heard nothing and the light did not appear again.

It was difficult to open the ammo box without making noise. He did it very slowly and carefully and hung the pistol in its holster over his shoulder. Then he climbed the slick clay bank, pulling himself up on exposed roots, taking care not to grab saplings, sure to shake if he touched them.

He found a game trail and followed it along the side of the river. Every now and then he stopped and listened, but there was no sound other than the rush of the river. Somewhere far off in the woods a whippoorwill called. The woods smelled of wet leaves from yesterday's rain. Briefly he caught the scent of some animal's scat.

Finally he reached a clump of cane and crept up into it until he could see the bridge. It was deserted. For a long time he knelt in the cane. His bad knee was starting to ache. The mosquitoes found him. He let them fill up with blood and fly away engorged. Someone could be standing twenty feet away hidden by the trees, ready to catch the movement of his hand and the sound of him swatting a mosquito. The air soon became thick with them, the insects making a wind of their own against his skin.

Something splashed in the river. It could have been a fish jumping or a snake dropping off a limb. He wished the person with the light would turn it on the sound. But there was nothing. A mosquito whined in his ear; he resisted the impulse to swat at it.

Instead of continuing down the bank, he circled back away from the river. That way he'd be sure of coming up behind the person with the light. If he were lucky, he'd see him silhouetted against the lighter darkness over the river.

It was easy to walk quietly on the wet leaves, which formed a soft, slick carpet beneath his feet. He moved slowly, pushing his way through single strands of silk spiders had spun across open spaces among the trees. He went down through a depression, filled with sand the river had dumped there during the last flood.

Then the land rose. He came up behind a clump of cane and saw, as he'd hoped, a figure outlined against the lighter darkness over the river. The man was standing still and watching the water. He held something in his hand. It glistened in the moonlight. A flashlight? He smelled bread. Maybe the man was fishing dough balls for carp.

Chalmers lost the bread scent. The man's hands moved, and whatever he held made a rustling sound. He crept forward. A slight breeze came off the river. He smelled the man's insect repellent but no scent of wintergreen tobacco. It wasn't Pick Dobine. Besides, he doubted whether Pick would have allowed anyone to sneak up on him. Pick spent so much time on the river that he had the senses of a deer or an otter. Instinct would have told him that Chalmers was in the woods behind him.

The whippoorwill called again, ten times, its calls beautifully regular. Chalmers took the safety off the pistol and took a step closer. He broke a twig. Instantly he went into a crouch, holding the pistol with both hands and training it on the man's back. Chalmers told himself he wouldn't be the first to shoot. But the man didn't move. Now he was certain it wasn't Pick Dobine or any other river man.

Chalmers took a few careful steps that brought him to within ten yards of the figure. Scattered low bushes grew in the sand. The path around them took him a little to the man's left. As Chalmers moved forward, the man turned toward him and a flashlight came on. Chalmers rolled out of the light and found safety behind a tree. He crouched low to the ground and brought up the pistol around the trunk.

"Back, devil!" a voice shouted.

The flashlight stabbed about in the darkness on both sides of the tree.

"Brother Sprott?" Chalmers asked.

"Yes, and God is with me," Brother Sprott said.

The preacher's voice was high-pitched, right on the edge of going out of control.

"It's Chalmers. Don't shoot."

"I am unarmed."

The preacher's voice was calmer now.

Chalmers stepped around the tree. Brother Sprott was holding a flashlight in one hand and an open Bible in the other. He held the Bible at arm's length. The flashlight illuminated the gilded pages and the red tassel.

"What're you doing here?" Chalmers asked.

"Waiting for midnight," Brother Sprott said.

Chalmers walked up on the riverbank and stood beside him.

"Why are you here?" Brother Sprott asked.

Chalmers noticed the preacher was still holding the Bible at arm's length between them. Perhaps he considered Chalmers a devil. Then Chalmers explained how he'd seen the light on the bridge.

They stood for a moment in silence. Chalmers scratched one of his mosquito bites.

"You out here after carp?" Chalmers asked.

He wanted to turn Brother Sprott away from the devil business.

"Devils," Brother Sprott said. "That woman has polluted this sacred pool. I have to cleanse it before we can baptize again here. She summons them here. When they come Jesus and I will defeat them."

"You seen any devils?"

"The flood was a sign from God."

"What about that one fifteen years ago? Was that a sign too? It washed away houses. Killed people."

"All is a sign from God. This whole world."

Brother Sprott swept his hand across the night sky.

"That woman is wicked, Chalmers," Brother Sprott said. "I saved you from the devil myself. Right down there by the bridge. You were born again. Come back to the Lord."

Brother Sprott was still holding his Bible in front of him as if it were a shield. Chalmers thought of Brother Sprott's father dying of the black lung; he thought of Brother Sprott helping his mother raise the younger children.

"You've got to stop saying those things about Livia," Chalmers said.

"The devil is leading you," Brother Sprott said. "For three days I have stood here. In the daytime and in the night. In the rain and in the sunlight. Devils will not pollute this spot. It belongs to the church. I will stand for four more days. The Lord gave me a sign. Praise the Lord."

Chalmers remembered how he'd pulled Livia out of the water by the bridge only a few months before. He recalled her diving naked for her sculptures in the pool.

"She won't come down here to swim again," Chalmers said.

"Maybe her body won't come," Brother Sprott said. "But her wicked soul will. Blazing, flaming with evil."

"You know that's not true," Chalmers said.

"She's lured you here. She means to destroy you."

"I'm here looking for folks stringing wire."

"Revenge is the Lord's, not yours."

"Then you and Livia are in agreement."

"You could've shot me with that pistol. The Lord would have forgave you, but that woman has hardened your heart against the Lord. You'd have died damned."

Chalmers realized it was no use arguing with Brother Sprott. It might be true he hadn't slept for three days. He'd see all the devils he desired, his exhausted mind stretched and baffled into hallucinations.

"She won't swim at this place again," Chalmers said. "I promise."

Brother Sprott reached out and took Chalmers by the shoulder. The man was trembling; he smelled of insect repellent and white bread. Then for the first time Chalmers noticed bread wrappers on the ground. That was what he'd seen glistening in the moonlight. A gallon milk container full of water was at Brother Sprott's feet. Bread and water for three days.

"Get away from her, Chalmers," Brother Sprott said. "Before it's too late."

Chalmers gently removed Brother Sprott's hand from his shoulder.

"You go on home," Chalmers said. "You keep wandering around here at night you're going step on a snake."

"Watch out for her!" Brother Sprott said. "Watch out!"

Chalmers gave up and walked off into the trees. Brother Sprott kept calling out after him.

Once in the canoe again, because of a tree that had fallen into the river, Chalmers was forced to paddle close to the bank where Brother Sprott was keeping his vigil. Brother Sprott put the light on him.

"You sleep with a Bible," Brother Sprott yelled. "It'll protect you from her. From her evil soul."

The flashlight swung back off Chalmers. For a moment Brother Sprott's face was illuminated by it. Then his face disappeared into the darkness, and the light was on the Bible he held in one hand. Brother Sprott began to read, something from Paul, Chalmers thought. The preacher's diet of bread and water along with no sleep was going to make him just as crazy as John David.

Chalmers went under the bridge and beached the canoe. Then he located the mountain bike and rode back to the truck. Livia had been right about the pistol. He could have shot Brother Sprott. He wished that he and Livia had come as strangers to Blount Country. That rich past, the web of kin going back all those generations, would be lost; but he and Livia could discover the river and Plumb's Bluff together. He smiled as he thought of going to the crossroad's store as a stranger.

But he could never be a stranger, no matter where he went in Blount Country. And Livia would always be feared, no matter how long she remained. There was no telling what Brother Sprott was going to stir up with his vigil. He'd end up seeing frightening things, and he'd terrorize the Nectar Bridge congregation with what he thought he'd seen, make them afraid too. When folks became afraid, they got dangerous.

CHAPTER FIFTEEN

Grandmother Rosa and Rudy Blount were going to be married. Everyone was surprised. She was still mad at Brother Sprott for his conduct toward Livia, so Grandmother Rosa had decided to bypass Brother Sprott and let a probate judge do the job. Madeline Williams, the judge, was a good friend. The wedding was three weeks away.

Livia decided to make a chess set for a wedding present. The river was Livia's theme. She made sketches of all the pieces. Pawns were catfish. Otters were bishops. Beavers were rooks. Knights were alligator snapping turtles. The queen was an egret and the king a great blue heron.

She made the kings first, one out of the black marble and the other out of the white stone. The figures were almost a foot high.

"My grandmother will have to get herself a bigger chess board," Chalmers observed.

Livia laughed.

"I make that too," Livia said.

She explained how she was going to lay a board made of colored tiles at the base of the big oak in his grandmother's yard.

"John David goes up and down in his tree," Livia said. "Your grandmother sits on the porch."

Chalmers imagined John David would be pleased with that arrangement.

When Livia finished the set she laid out the tiles by the picnic table. She and Chalmers played. She beat him in five moves.

"You should play with my grandmother," he said.

Instead of going to Susan Moore, Livia invited Grandmother Rosa and John David out to Plumb's Bluff. Livia presented her with the set, which Livia planned to install the day before the wedding.

Grandmother Rosa was delighted. John David took a knight up into a tree with him. She shouted up at him until he brought it back and placed it on the board.

They played that first game one Saturday afternoon while Chalmers watched. He had just come up from running the gates. Livia managed to beat his grandmother, but John David quickly won his game.

That began several days of games. Now, because the days were longer, Chalmers was paddling after he came home from work while the others played chess. Livia had made no progress on the marble plug. The bow of the canoe was emerging from the block of marble but that was all. Chalmers had resigned himself to racing one of his own designs at the end of the summer.

They often played on into the evening. When it grew dark, they turned on the string of lights. Livia had painted the bulbs different colors. Reds and greens and purples and yellows fell on the tiles and on the faces of the animal chess pieces. The cicadas whined from the trees, and John David, whether he was playing or not, went on with his ceaseless climbing.

John David had set a spider's web of ropes over the river, a series of Tyrolean traverses. Chalmers would be concentrating on a gate and suddenly John David would appear a few feet above it, sometimes hanging upside down. But Chalmers discovered, to his surprise, that concentrating on blocking out the antics of John David actually made his runs better. So instead of worrying about taking the wrong angle into an eddy, he tried to use his paddler's instincts to find the perfect angle instead of attempting to calculate it. Once when John David hung so low Chalmers had to duck his head to pass under him, Chalmers made a particularly smooth pass through a gate. Chalmers heard John David laughing as he headed for the downstream gate, the current pushing him away from it, but again, somehow, he found a good angle and went through it smoothly.

Gradually their chess games developed into a tournament. Livia had figured out John David's style of play and was coming up with strategies that gave him trouble. John David would swing down from a tree and discover Livia making moves he hadn't seen before. But John David held onto his lead.

Chalmers had paddled until it was almost dark. As he walked up the trail with the canoe over his shoulder, he guessed John David was getting beat by Livia because he'd stayed off the ropes over the river. Occasionally Chalmers had seen him in the treetops, his movements partially illuminated by the colored lights. Chalmers wondered if he could hire John David to hang upside down over the course in North Carolina.

He reached the picnic table. John David had just made his move and had returned to the tree. Chalmers heard the clicks of the climbing irons. Livia was studying the board; she'd castled. John David was attacking with a knight, threatening her queen's bishop.

Grandmother Rosa walked with Chalmers as he put the canoe on the rack by the shop

"Guess I'll be working for you after Sunday," he said.

"Not really," she said. "It'll be awhile before we combine everything. But we have to do that. It doesn't make sense to compete against each other."

Livia sat in the pool of colored light studying the board, the clock ticking on the table.

"Chalmers, she can't stay here," Grandmother Rosa said.

"She won't go near the Nectar Pool," Chalmers said.

"That's not the point. Macon went too far. Then there was that flood."

"Let Brother Sprott pack up and leave."

Somewhere, not so deep beneath all of her talk, Chalmers suspected, was her interest, now combined with Rudy's, in the land. He could imagine her thinking he'd go with Livia, and before long the power of the promise he'd made would fade. He'd forget the seriousness of it. In the end he'd sell.

"Be reasonable," she said. "Someone is going to hurt her. Then you'll hurt somebody and wind up in prison. I don't want that."

"She won't be any more trouble," Chalmers insisted.

But he knew that his grandmother might be right. Livia was always going to do what she wanted. She'd promised to stay away from the Nectar Bridge, but one night on an impulse she might go there to swim. She was fearless. If she understood what some of the people in the county were like, she wouldn't be that way. But it seemed that making her understand exactly how things were in Blount Country was impossible. He'd compared the county to Romania. Told her that the same sort of terrible things could happen. She laughed at that.

"This is America," Livia had said. "No Securitate."

John David appeared to make his move. He talked with Livia for a moment before he put his hand on a piece. Then he went back up the tree.

"Just wait to the end of the summer and the Nationals," Chalmers said. "I win and I won't be blasting any more."

"I hope so," she said. "You could make canoes in Tennessee or North Carolina. It doesn't have to be here."

"Livia!" John David's high-pitched voice came from a tree-top.

Chalmers heard the hiss of the rope through John David's figure-eight rappelling device.

Livia looked up into the tree and put her finger to her lips.

John David came down hard on the ground beside her. He was saying something Chalmers couldn't understand.

Bark flew from the tree beside Livia's head, followed by the flat sound of a rifle echoing off the bluff. John David threw her to the ground. The window of the trailer shattered. Next was the windshield of Livia's van. By now Chalmers had pulled his grandmother to the ground and was shielding her with his body. Then the hidden rifleman shot out one of the colored lights. The bulb exploded, a fine spray of glass raining down on them.

Chalmers listened to his grandmother's rapid breathing. She was making no other sound but that. She smelled of flowers.

"Don't move," Chalmers said.

He stood up. A clear picture sprung into his mind of his father's body caught on the wire. There was no more shooting. He got to his feet and started across the yard. It was as if he were moving in a dream at slow time. Livia was motioning for him to get down. John David simply watched. Chalmers strode to the edge of the bluff and stopped, looking across at the line of dark trees.

"Go ahead, you bastard!" he yelled.

His words echoed into the darkness. There was a silence.

"Chalmers?" Livia shouted.

He ignored her.

"Shoot me!" he screamed. "Here I am! Shoot me!"

He'd counted four shots. It was reasonable to expect that the rifleman had more in the magazine.

"Chalmers!" Livia screamed. "Please!"

He turned and saw she was getting to her feet.

"Stay down!" he said.

She crouched by the table. He turned back to face the darkness.

"Shoot, dammit, shoot!" Chalmers shouted.

He felt Livia's hands on him. She was pulling him away from the edge of the bluff. Then they had their backs to the tree. John David, a smile on his face, regarded them from under the picnic table.

"Stay here, Chalmers!" Livia gasped. "Please!"

Chalmers looked across to the shop. His grandmother was sitting on the ground. John David came out from under the table and darted across the open space, his hardware jingling. For the first time Chalmers considered what it meant to present himself as a clear target to the rifleman. But from the second shot he'd sensed the person wasn't shooting to kill.

"What are you doing, Chalmers?" Livia asked.

"I don't know," he said. "Thinking of my daddy, I guess."

"We will go to Mobile," she said.

"No, we're not going to Mobile. We're going to my grandmother's wedding. Then to North Carolina. Then back here to build boats."

Chalmers was surprised by his words. Livia was in danger. He could eliminate that danger by leaving. Yet he was talking of staying. He felt himself trembling. He stepped out from behind the tree.

"We're not leaving!" he shouted. "Livia stays! I stay!"

In reply he heard only the sound of his voice echoing off the trees.

Grandmother Rosa was standing beside him.

"I'll go call the sheriff," she said.

She started toward the trailer, but he took her arm.

"Later," Chalmers said. "He can come over anytime and dig that bullet out of my living room wall. Won't find a thing over in the woods. They got any sense they'll get rid of the rifle."

"I warned you," Grandmother Rosa said. "You've got to take responsibility for this girl."

"You still want us to run?" Chalmers asked.

"No, I want you to stay," Grandmother Rosa said. "I want you at my wedding." She put her arm around Livia. "You can stay at my house tonight."

"We're staying here," Chalmers said.

"I'm afraid, Chalmers," Grandmother Rosa said.

"So am I," Chalmers said. "This is my home. Nobody's gonna make me leave."

"Exactly what your father would've said," Grandmother Rosa observed.

Now they all sat on the picnic table. Chalmers looked at the shattered window in his trailer and the bullet hole in the windshield of Livia's van. There was a dark gap in the string of lights. John David pushed a piece of light bulb off the table. The cicadas whined from the trees; the river rushed against the rocks. For a long time no one said anything.

Finally Livia stood up and walked to the chess pieces. For some reason the memory of a lover in Bucharest came to her mind. They were in an apartment in the old city, on the banks of the Danube. She was standing at the window, and he was standing behind her, his hands on her breasts. And she was watching the boats strung with colored lights pass on the river, a sight that caused her to ignore those familiar hands.

She'd tried to drown herself. Why should she worry about a few rifle shots? She bent over and moved a pawn to threaten John David's knight.

"You're going to lose your bishop," Chalmers said.

"I know," she said.

She set the clock in motion. It began to tick. The sound seemed to Chalmers louder than the cicadas. He supposed this was simply because of the pitch to which he'd raised himself. It didn't seem possible to him now that he'd stood on the edge of the bluff and screamed at the rifleman. Probably the man was long gone before he even started yelling.

John David walked over to the board and moved his bishop.

"Excellent, excellent," Livia whispered.

"Three moves to check," Grandmother Rosa said.

Livia punched the clock for herself.

Grandmother Rosa was wrong. Instead of three moves it took six. Chalmers could tell that John David was frustrated by Livia's tactics.

While John David was waiting for Livia to make her last move and then checkmate her, Chalmers walked over to the van. The bullet had gone through the window at an angle. He opened the door and found the hole it had made in the top of the driver's seat. He opened the rear doors and turned on the light. The van was filled with tools. The cot where Livia slept for so long was placed along one wall. Ivan and Phoebe stood on the other side. For some reason Phoebe's shiny black thorax looked as if it had increased in size, turning her into a pregnant insect. But when he took a step closer he realized this was an illusion created by the light.

He sat on the end of the cot next to the driver's seat exit hole made by the bullet and tried to guess from the angle where it might be. It appeared that it must have gone close to the statues. He ran his hand over Ivan's feathers, searching for a hole. Ivan smelled musty. A thin layer of dust was on his feathers. Then he did the same with Phoebe. Not even a scratch on her thorax.

He went down on his hands and knees and looked among the tools and pieces of marble. Then, between Ivan's yellow feet, he saw it. The bullet was only slightly deformed. It felt solid and heavy as he hefted it. He'd turn it over to the sheriff in the morning.

As he looked at the statues, he imagined all those nights Livia had slept in the van alone. He wondered if she had imaginary conversations with Phoebe.

Chalmers considered whether his insistence about staying at Plumb's Bluff made him as grotesque as the statues. It made sense to get Livia out of the county. But he didn't think he could leave the land; he didn't think he could send her away. Besides, whoever had strung wire in the river was still out there somewhere. For all he knew it was the same person with the rifle.

"Chalmers?"

Livia stood at the end of the van, framed by the darkness behind her.

"John David wins," she said.

"That's no surprise," he said.

She laughed.

Then she climbed into the van and sat on the cot beside him. He held out the bullet in his open hand.

"For the sheriff," he said.

She threw her arms around him. He wanted to hold onto her all night. They sat on the cot for a long time, their arms wrapped about each other until Chalmers heard the jingling sound that meant John David was standing in the doorway.

Chalmers looked up to see John David's grinning face.

"Come on," Chalmers said. "We'll take my grandmother home."

CHAPTER SIXTEEN

Grandmother Rosa did not invite many people to the wedding. They'd decided to hold it at her house in Susan Moore. She told Chalmers how she and Rudy had argued over whether Chalmers and Livia should come. But Rudy hadn't reacted as violently to the shooting as Chalmers thought he might.

"I don't want nobody shooting up our wedding," Rudy had said.

Finally he'd relented. Rudy had insisted on wearing a pistol in a shoulder holster under his jacket. Chalmers wasn't carrying. But he'd put the .44 under the driver's seat in the van. He hadn't been able to keep the pistol out of the van, despite his promise to himself. Now, when he went to the crossroad's store, he made it a point to be especially polite to everyone. And no matter how much someone provoked him, he wasn't going to be drawn into a fight. But he felt helpless without the pistol.

He and Livia argued about that.

"They will shoot from far away," Livia said. "You will shoot back?"

"It makes me feel safe," he said. "And who knows what somebody'll do. You want me to take them on with a tire iron?"

"Give our protection to the sheriff," she said.

The sheriff and his deputies had been out to look at the bullet holes. Livia was gone to Birmingham when they came. They'd walked the woods on the other side of the river searching for shell casings. They'd found nothing. But they had the bullet. That would be enough if the rifle ever turned up.

"You get that woman out of this county," the sheriff had said.

It seemed to Chalmers that everyone was telling him the same thing.

"She's got as much right as anybody to be here," Chalmers had said.

"True," the sheriff said. "I'll have a deputy keep an eye on your place. But I've only got a few deputies. This is a big county. Can't keep a man out here forever."

"Don't need a man out here."

"Suit yourself. Can't that woman go back to Romania?"

"She lives here. She's an American."

"Don't look like any American to me."

"Go someplace besides Birmingham sometime."

The sheriff laughed.

"People around here won't ever think of her as an American," he said. "So you be sure to turn the lights off at night. Don't go making yourselves targets."

"You go talk with Brother Sprott."

"I have. He's all full of being free to do what he wants too. But he ain't free to incite folks to do harm to that woman. I told him that if anything happens to her, he's the first one I'll come looking for."

"Not many votes in that."

"That's like something your daddy'd say."

"That's true."

Chalmers liked being compared to his father.

"Leave it alone, Chalmers. I don't think we're ever gonna find who strung that wire. You go on off and win your race. Get that woman out of this county. You sure you don't want a deputy out this way for a few days? Might discourage whoever did that shooting."

"No thanks."

Then the sheriff had driven off, the fishing pole antenna on the dust-covered car swaying. Chalmers had looked around the yard, the birds singing in the trees. No place he knew was more peaceful. It made him even more determined that after the race he'd come back with Livia. They'd get married. Raise children at Plumb's Bluff. Chalmers imagined himself teaching his son to paddle.

Livia drove them to the wedding in her van. What was left of Chalmers' truck was sitting in the yard. It was badly damaged from the flood. He'd pulled the engine out and was planning on rebuilding it after the race.

They went up the walk. John David was sitting on the first huge limb of the oak.

"Play with me?" John David asked.

Livia shook her head. John David went up into the tree.

Livia had come over and installed the chess set under the tree. The pieces were arranged in order on the red and black tiles. Edward and his parents were among the people on the porch. Chalmers hadn't seen much of him because Edward's father had got him on at the steel mill in Birmingham. Edward was working third shift.

Chalmers introduced Livia to his and Rudy's relatives. They were all polite to her.

"I been asking around," Edward said. "Nobody knows who done that shooting."

"Brother Sprott knows," Chalmers said.

"Maybe. I brought a pistol. Case somebody tries to start trouble."

Chalmers wondered if he was the only one besides Livia and John David who wasn't armed. Maybe even Madeline Williams had a small .32 caliber automatic tucked away in her purse.

"Nothing's going to happen," Chalmers said.

And he was proved right, for the wedding, held in the living room, which always smelled musty from the ancient carpets and overstuffed chairs, went off smoothly. Lottie Jones played an old piano whose veneer was cracked. John David hung on a rope and watched through an open window.

Afterwards Chalmers stood on the porch and drank punch and ate cake.

Livia was talking with John David again. They stood next to the chess set.

"Chalmers in the moonlight," John David said. "Chalmers in the moonlight. Moonlight shining on that big pistol."

"It is an obsession," Livia said.

"Randall Plumb found out what's at the bottom of the river. Catfish, snakes, crayfish, minnows, snakes—old tires."

John David paused and looked up into the tree. Livia didn't follow his eyes.

"Miss Rosa is dreaming of that coal," John David continued.

"I hear her groaning in the night. That coal is laying heavy on her. You got to tell Chalmers to sell."

"He will never sell," Livia said. "He says he will never leave the river."

"Then he'll wind up down there talking to catfish."

"He stops paddling at night. He stops."

John David shook his head.

"I do believe he lies down in that grave with his daddy every night."

John David reached up and tugged on a rope. A jay screamed from the treetop.

"I strung that wire," John David announced calmly. "I strung it and he paddled himself right onto it. Danced on the wire for a little while but then he was still."

Liva turned and looked at Chalmers standing on the porch. He smiled at her; she waved to him.

"A dream?" Livia asked.

"No dream," John David said. "Chalmers'll be dancing on the wire if he don't sell soon."

Liva wondered if it was she who was in a dream. John David, who'd just calmly announced that he'd murdered Randall Plumb, was grinning at her.

"The sheriff—" Livia began

"He'll just say that it was me talking wild," John David said. "But I ain't crazy. I just like trees. I dance in trees, not on a piece of wire."

Then, with a click of climbing irons, John David ascended and vanished into the leaves.

Livia felt herself shaking. But she knew that Chalmers was watching. Through a great effort of will she turned and walked onto the porch.

She took the punch cup out of his hand and had a drink.

"What's wrong?" Chalmers asked.

"John David thinks they shoot me," she said.

Chalmers laughed.

"Nothing's going happen to you."

"You could sell your land."

"In a year I'll be making canoes there."

"You can make them anywhere."

Rudy came up to them.

"Come on, Chalmers," he said. "We gonna shoot bottles at the railroad cut. Every man at this wedding and some women came armed. Ain't that something?"

"You go on," Chalmers said. "We won't miss it."

Rudy left along with the rest of the people on the porch. John David lowered himself into view and stared at them. Then he went back up into the tree.

"Let your grandmother have the land," Livia said.

Chalmers wondered if Grandmother Rosa had been working on Livia.

"We will go to the place where you race," she said. "You will build your factory there."

"You know what they'd do to that land?" Chalmers asked.

"You work at the mine. No more than what you are doing."

Chalmers imagined the cut rippling as the charges went off.

Out back they'd begun to shoot. Chalmers heard the pop of the pistols and laughter.

"Trees will grow again," Livia said.

Chalmers knew that was true. Trees would eventually grow back, except on a few scattered spots of sterile or toxic soil. The spill would surely silt up the river, but that too could recover. Yet the topography of the land would be changed forever.

"I promised," Chalmers said.

"You must forget," she said.

The pistols popped again. There was more laughter.

"I can't."

"Yes, you take your pistol on the river. In a year, in two nothing left of Chalmers Plumb. Nothing for me to love."

She was crying now.

Chalmers heard the jingle of John David's carabineers. He was on the ground moving the chess pieces about.

"I love you, Chalmers," she said. "Why must you love dirt and rocks and trees."

"It's my land," Chalmers said.

He thought of all the charges he'd set, of all the days he'd watched the dragline taking huge bites out of the earth. In a few months what was a few rolling hills had been rearranged into tall piles of spill and steep gullies.

"Please, Chalmers," she said. "This is a place for your destruction."

"We're going to North Carolina at the end of the summer," Chalmers said.

"Never come back?"

"You stay away from the Nectar Bridge and everything'll be all right."

"We go to Mobile? After you race."

"Maybe."

Chalmers was sure his grandmother had been talking with Livia.

"You must forget," Livia said.

The last time he'd seen her this upset was that first day he set eyes on her at Nectar Pool. Tears ran down her cheeks.

"I won't take the pistol on the river again," he said.

"You promise?"

"Yes."

"Even when I am in Birmingham."

"Yes."

"Give it away?"

Chalmers wasn't sure he was going to do that. At least not until the people Brother Sprott had stirred up had a chance to calm down.

Livia put her hand on his arm.

"Forget your father's death," she said. "Revenge is bad. It will destroy you."

"I know," Chalmers said.

"Good. Good."

"Get the pistol. Give it to Rudy Blount."

Chalmers went to the truck for the pistol. They walked around to the back of the house where the wedding party was shooting at bottles and cans set on a sandstone ledge in the side of the railroad cut.

Grandmother Rosa was shooting a .25 caliber semi-automatic. She fired five times and missed all the bottles. The gun made a quick series of pops that reminded Chalmers of a cap pistol. Madeline was laughing at her.

Chalmers handed the pistol to Rudy.

"Another wedding present," Chalmers said.

"Livia! Livia!" John David called.

Everyone turned to witness John David speaking. He was in the very top of the oak tree. The thin branch on which he stood swayed back and forth under him.

"Go down!" Grandmother Rosa shouted. "Go down!"

She waved her arm in going down motions.

John David grinned and waved. Everyone laughed.

"Like a squirrel," Rudy said. Then he turned back to Chalmers. "That's your daddy's pistol."

"I got no use for it," Chalmers said.

"Thank you, Chalmers," Grandmother Rosa said.

She took the pistol, which was in its holster, out of his hand and handed it to Rudy.

"The sheriff can't keep you safe at Plumb's Bluff," Rudy said.

"No pistol at the river," Livia said.

"Mighty foolish," Rudy said. "Somebody could just walk right in there and—"

"Hush, Rudy," Grandmother Rosa interrupted.

Rudy looked at Grandmother Rosa.

"A fine pistol," Rudy said.

He turned to the unbroken bottles. Rudy held the pistol with two hands and carefully broke the four bottles. Everyone clapped. John David whistled from the top of the tree. He'd moved down to a slightly larger branch.

Most of them returned to the house leaving Edward and two other men to shoot. Pretty soon the men got tired of shooting bottles and everyone went home. John David came down from the tree.

Chalmers stood on the porch. John David moved the chess pieces about, playing chess with himself. But he soon tired of that. He arranged them on their proper squares and went up into the tree. Rudy came out on the porch. He held the pistol in his hand.

"You take this," Rudy said as he handed Chalmers the pistol.

Chalmers shook his head.

"No, don't you argue," Rudy said "You need it."

Chalmers was thankful to have the pistol back. He went out to the van and put it under the seat. He'd hide it in the trailer when they returned home.

As Chalmers came up the walk to Livia and Grandmother Rosa, who'd just stepped out on the porch, he heard John David making squirrel noises from his perch in the top of the oak tree. Chalmers wondered if John David would tell Livia about the pistol or if he'd even noticed Rudy pressing it into his hands.

"Livia!" John David called. "Livia!"

Chalmers lowered his eyes and walked to the porch where the women waited.

CHAPTER SEVENTEEN

Chalmers stayed away from Plumb's Run on moonlit nights but found the habit hard to break. He and Livia did not speak of his avoidance of the river. He looked forward to cloudy nights or a waning moon. Then it was easier not to think of wire in Plumb's Run, of sitting in his boat in the eddy behind the big rock. Waiting.

Livia was carving wood now. She'd gotten her hands on some cypress stumps and logs. She was making sketches, but she wouldn't let Chalmers see them. When he came home from the mine, she'd be sitting at the table working on a big pad, crumpled sheets of discarded paper scattered on the ground like the fallen blossoms of a tulip tree. Chalmers hoped she wasn't going to make any more of the toothed figures.

John David no longer came to the river to play chess with Livia. She went to Grandmother Rosa's. Chalmers didn't think that Rudy would tolerate John David there much longer. Who would want some forty-year-old man up and down a tree outside their bedroom window?

Livia had gone to play chess at Susan Moore one evening. Chalmers was sitting at the picnic table reading a book when Pick Dobine drove his truck into the yard. Pick had never delivered the catfish he'd promised. Chalmers supposed that at last he was getting around to it.

"Brought us some catfish?" Chalmers asked.

Pick shook his head. Pick looked worried, like a lost hound come up out of a swamp to stand forlornly by the side of a the road, waiting for a familiar pickup to appear.

"I know you didn't string that wire," Chalmers said.

"I didn't, my kin didn't," Pick said.

They stood by Pick's truck. He'd been running his trap line. Two dead otters lay stiff on the metal floor.

"I been checking my lines," Pick said. "I come through Mr. Karl's pasture. Where Wilson Creek goes into the river. Above Skirum Bluff."

"I know the place," Chalmers said.

The creek came into the river not far above Plumb's Run.

"Somebody cut wire on Mr. Karl's pasture. All that new wire he strung last week. Cows are down in the woods. Gonna lose a cow in the river. I reckon they're stringing in the river. This time they got 'em enough to put up a three-strand fence. They mean for somebody to die. Tonight'll be a good night for stringing wire."

"Who?"

"Ain't none of my kin."

"You don't know that."

"I'd know. They'd ask me to help. They ain't asked."

Pick helped him put the boat in the water. Chalmers lashed the ammo box containing the pistol to a thwart.

"You want me to call the sheriff?" Pick asked.

"No," Chalmers said.

Now the memories of his father hanging on the wire came flooding into his mind.

He gave himself up to them. He couldn't live by Livia's philosophy.

"I'd shoot 'em," Pick said. "Save the county the expense of a trial." Pick laughed. "Besides, it kind of makes a Dobine uneasy calling the law. Usually it's the other way around." Pick again laughed, the sound like the chattering call of a kingfisher.

It was a hour or so until dark. Chalmers guessed he could reach Plumb's Run in forty minutes.

"You watch yourself," Pick said.

Chalmers promised he would.

He went down the river in the gathering darkness. He considered how correct what he was going to do would be according to Dobine morality. Dobines would regard his actions as ones of the highest virtue. Grandmother Rosa and Livia would have other views. He wondered what Rudy Blount would think.

It was almost dark when he reached Plumb's Run. The evening star hung over the ridge, but the moon was not up yet. He went down through the rapid. At the first drop, the easy one, he almost made a mistake. The upstream gunwale dipped as he prepared to make a turn, and he took on some water but not enough to prevent him from finding the safety of an eddy. As he bailed out the boat, he told himself he'd be fine as long as he concentrated.

The rest of the run went smoothly. As the moon rose over the ridge, he took the boat into the eddy behind the big rock. He paddled the boat into the crack, took the pistol out of the ammo box, and waited.

He sat in the eddy for a long time, waiting for a canoe to suddenly appear in the eddy or for someone to walk down to the water. He still wasn't sure what he would do if they were carrying wire. He hoped they were armed. That would make it easy, especially if they shot first. He decided he wouldn't fire unless they shot first or ran.

But after a couple of hours, he began to wonder if anyone was going to try to string wire at this place or this night. So he went down through the rapid. At a bend he turned the bow of the canoe upstream to make a ferry across to midstream eddy, his back to the difficult drop below. He reached the eddy and turned to look downstream to check the line he should take to approach the drop.

And there, standing above the drop, which was not more than thirty yards away, in what to Chalmers looked like midair, was John David. His back was to Chalmers. He was naked, wearing only his climbing harness.

Chalmers looked closer and saw John David was balanced on a rope. He'd anchored one end to a pine of Chalmers' side of the river and the other to a poplar the opposite bank. He'd strung another rope parallel to the rope and about chest high. John David had one hand on the rope and the other on a piece of wire. He was pulling wire, also anchored to the pine, across the rapid. The wire had returned to its coiled state. It hadn't been on the fence long enough for the steel to lose the memory of the coil. The wire seemed to have a life of its own as it dangled in tight coils above the water. Chalmers took the boat out of the eddy and ferried it to the bank. He removed the pistol from its box and worked his way through a stand of river birches to where John David had tied rope and wire to the pine.

Chalmers stepped out on a boulder. John David had his attention fixed on the wire and the opposite bank. Chalmers remembered his father caught on the wire. He clearly saw Randall Plumb's arm rising and falling as the current surged against it. He brought up the pistol on John David. As he did, Chalmers thought of all of Livia's warnings. She would never forgive him for killing John David. The sights wandered off John David, even though Chalmers held the pistol with two hands. Chalmers wondered what John David was thinking, why he was doing it. Chalmers resisted the impulse to call out. He brought the sights back on him, trying hard to control his shaking hands.

Then suddenly John David was bathed in light, his figure transfixed, the light shining off the new wire and the row of carabineers John David wore on his harness. The light revealed he was weaving a web of wire in the rapid. There was a long cut on his arm, probably from wrestling with the wire.

"Goddamn, it's John David!" Pick Dobine yelled.

Pick was standing on the boulder only a few yards away. Then Pick played his light over Chalmers.

"Shoot him, Chalmers!" Pick yelled.

The light was on John David again.

John David held the wire in his hand. The steel coils bobbed in the light, like a giant spring. He stood casually on the rope, steadying himself with one hand on the other rope. Chalmers was reminded of cartoons in which characters performed antics in disregard of the laws of physics. John David looked into the light and smiled.

"Kill him!" Pick yelled. "I told you it weren't no Dobine."

John David walked farther out over the rapid. Pick played his light over John David.

"He put your daddy on the wire," Pick said. "Ain't but one thing to do."

John David studied the water below.

"Shoot the son-of-a-bitch!" Pick yelled.

John David sat down on the rope.

"Thinks he's in the circus," Pick said.

John David sat balanced on the rope and adjusted the wire, trying to shake the coils out of it.

Up on the ridge Chalmers saw lights and heard voices.

"The sheriff," Pick said. "Do it now!"

Someone else, probably Mr. Karl, had discovered the cut

fence and reported it.

Chalmers brought the pistol up. And again he thought of explaining what he was about to do to Livia.

"He killed your daddy," Pick said. "Sheriff gets here and it'll be too late."

Chalmers thought of Livia. Somehow he couldn't imagine putting his hands on her if he shot John David. Chalmers lowered the pistol.

A powerful light from the sheriff's men fell upon John David. John David got to his feet and stood frozen on the rope. He turned away from his task to look at them.

"Get off!" Chalmers yelled.

Then another light was on him. Men shouted to each other. Chalmers heard them moving through the underbrush, followed by the sound of their boots on the rocks. It seemed to Chalmers that John David was about to speak.

"Livia!" he shouted.

The sound of his shrill voice was mostly lost in the rush of the river. He raised his arm that held the wire, and the wire twisted below him like a thing alive, looping in tight coils.

"Hook yourself up!" Chalmers shouted.

Now there were lights playing over him from every direction.

"Look at that damn wire," a voice called.

"Thinks he's a spider," another voice said.

John David looped the wire over the rope.

"Livia!" John David called again.

And Chalmers half expected her to reply.

"Come off that rope!" the sheriff shouted.

"Shoot him!" Pick screamed. "Shoot him!"

"Shut your damn mouth," the sheriff said.

Pick was silent.

"Come over here, John David," the sheriff yelled. "Nobody's gonna hurt you."

"Livia Tarna Mare!" John David yelled.

John David began to bounce on the rope. Chalmers had seen him play that game before on a limb, high up in a tree.

"Careful," the sheriff yelled.

A coil of wire suddenly snaked around John David's neck. He grabbed at it and dropped off the rope. They all heard the sound of his body falling into the water. Then there was just the rush of the water. A man cursed. The wire tied to the pine swung downstream as it absorbed the weight of his body.

"Just like a big catfish on my line," Pick said.

Chalmers returned the pistol to its holster and slung it over his shoulder.

"Turtle meat, boys," Pick said. "Turtle meat."

Some of the men laughed nervously, but most were silent. Like Chalmers they looked at the water, illuminated by their lights, flowing swift and foam-flecked over the rocks. He imagined John David at the bottom of the river, free from whatever had driven him to string the wire, his naked body floating limp in its stiff, barbed embrace.

CHAPTER EIGHTEEN

The sheriff dropped Chalmers off at Grandmother Rosa's. Every light was on, the house perched on the side of the railroad cut, a beacon to approaching trains. Music was playing, a woman's voice singing a sad song. As Chalmers went up the walk, he thought of how many times John David had called to him from the top of the big oak.

Rudy and Grandmother Rosa and Livia came out on the porch. Chalmers supposed Grandmother Rosa and Livia had been playing chess. Rudy must have been glad when he discovered John David had gone off somewhere.

"I turn around and there's John David, hanging outside my window," Rudy had become fond of saying. "I don't know how Rosa has stood it all these years."

"What you doing with the sheriff?" Rudy asked.

Rudy came down off the porch and out of the light.

"John David was stringing wire," Chalmers said.

"Goddamn," Rudy said.

Grandmother Rosa made a sound, but it wasn't speech. She stood very straight and tall. It seemed to Chalmers as if she were gazing at him from a great height.

Livia came down the steps. She put her arms around him. Chalmers found he was shaking again.

"He's dead," Chalmers said.

Chalmers spoke the words softly so only Rudy and Livia heard. Rudy turned and looked at Grandmother Rosa who had just stepped off the porch.

"Not you?" Livia said. "Please it not be you."

Scott Ely

"No," Chalmers said. "Not that way."

Livia began to sob.

"The wire got him," Chalmers said. "It wasn't me."

"Come up here and tell me," Grandmother Rosa said.

Rudy had walked up to stand with her. He put his hand on her arm. Together, like a pair of dancers, they took a step backwards onto the porch. Dragonflies and moths swarmed about a naked bulb dropped down from the ceiling on an piece of wire. Occasionally there was a tinkling sound as the insects bumped into it. A heavy moth crashed into the screen.

Chalmers walked up and stood before her.

"Tell me," she said.

She was trembling. Rudy put one of his big hands on her shoulder. She took it and pressed the back of his hand against her cheek.

"John David was stringing wire," Chalmers said.

"And you?" she asked.

"I didn't shoot him," Chalmers said. "He fell in the river. Tangled in the wire. Drowned."

"Randall?"

"I guess John David strung that wire. We'll never know for sure."

"He did it," Livia said.

They all turned to look at her.

"He tells me," Livia said.

Chalmers thought of making love to Livia in the canoe and how the light had been diffused by the translucent hull and turned into a softness that illuminated her breasts. Even then she might have known and had kept silent.

"Why?" Rudy asked.

"Because of me," Grandmother Rosa said.

She had sat down heavily in a rocking chair.

"I wanted Randall's land," she said.

"You told him to string wire?" Chalmers asked.

Rudy stepped closer to Grandmother Rosa.

"No," Grandmother Rosa said. "But he heard me complain every day that I wanted it."

"He wasn't right in the head," Rudy said. "He couldn't make any sense out of that."

"Different," Grandmother Rosa said. "That's all he was."

She was crying now. A single tear caught the light as it slid down her cheek.

"It's like I strung that wire myself," she said. "If I hadn't been so greedy then Randall would be alive. John David would be alive."

"Hush," Rudy said.

Grandmother Rosa looked like a rag doll sprawled in the rocker, she who always sat with perfect posture, her spine never touching the back of a chair.

"Dead!" she cried. "I killed my own son! Who will forgive me?"

Chalmers imagined that Brother Sprott would tell her that Jesus would forgive her, but Chalmers kept that thought to himself.

"You didn't kill nobody," Rudy said angrily. "John David did. Now he's dead. It's over."

"For coal," she said. "I did it for coal."

Livia was kneeling beside her, her arm around Rosa's shoulder.

"Come inside," Livia said.

"Yes, you go make her a drink," Rudy said. "She needs a drink."

"I think if I have a drink I'll be all right," Grandmother Rosa said.

Livia took Grandmother Rosa into the house.

"I ain't sorry John David is dead," Rudy said. "They'd put him in the hospital in Tuscaloosa. Wouldn't let him climb trees. It'd be like living in hell for him."

Chalmers wasn't sorry either, only thankful he hadn't followed Pick's prompting and shot John David. He remembered the feel of the trigger against his finger as he brought up the sights on John David. Chalmers had taken the slack out of the trigger. He'd come that close. He imagined John David's body lying at the bottom of the river.

"Don't matter what we think," Chalmers said. "He's dead."

"How'd Livia know?" Rudy said.

Chalmers explained how he'd watched them talking together. Livia had known then. She'd been afraid that Chalmers would find out. He imagined how frightened for him she must have been every time he ran the river with the pistol in the canoe. She must have been talking with John David about the wire, trying to persuade him never to string any again.

"He told her," Chalmers said.

Chalmers tried to imagine how bad that must have been for her, the moment when she realized that John David had murdered Randall Plumb.

"She should've told somebody," Rudy said.

"Maybe," Chalmers said.

"Don't see how that could've hurt."

"She could've promised not to tell."

Chalmers thought of Livia's response to her murdered family, her belief in forgetting. He could imagine her deciding the best thing to do would be to convince John David he shouldn't string wire.

"Brother Sprott'll be over here before long," Rudy said. "It's not a good time for you two to tangle."

They went into the house. Livia and Grandmother Rosa were sitting at the kitchen table. Rosa had a glass of whiskey and ice in her hands.

"We've got to go," Chalmers said. "Brother Sprott'll be coming."

"Stay and make your peace with him," Grandmother Rosa said.

"No peace to be made," Chalmers said. "He'd been satisfied if that wire had gotten me."

"Do you forgive me, Chalmers?" Grandmother Rosa asked.

"Wasn't your fault."

"I just said to John David that I wished Randall would sell," she said. "I said I was angry with you. That I wanted you to sell."

Chalmers put his arms around her. She felt frail in his arms and smelled of whiskey.

"It's nobody's fault," Chalmers said. "Nobody's fault."

"That John David was crazy," Rudy said. "You go on, Chalmers."

Chalmers went out of the house with Livia. Soon it would fill with kin who would come bringing food, the smells of chicken and pies and cakes and cornbread filling the house.

On the way down the walk Livia turned and looked up at John David's tree.

"You are not angry?" she asked.

"No," he said.

He pulled her close to him.

"It's not your fault," he said.

"He was very good at chess," she said.

"Yes."

"The emperor of trees."

"That he was."

"Chalmers, I could never tell you."

"Why?"

"Because you cannot forget. A trap in your mind has caught you."

"Well, it's over now."

"Will you love your grandmother?"

"Yes."

"Good."

They reached the van.

"I work in cypress now," she said. "You will like."

"Not terrible beautiful?" he asked.

"Only if I am led that way."

Chalmers recalled that first time he'd seen her, standing on the bridge flanked by Ivan and Phoebe.

"You make what you want," he said. "You make what you have to."

"I make soft things," she said. "Terrible but soft."

He laughed.

"I want to see that," he said.

She drove them to the river. The headlights fell on the pieces of cypress as they came into the yard.

"We will stay here?" she asked.

"Forever," he said.

"I could not tell you of John David."

"I know."

He pulled her close to him and kissed her. She was crying. He hoped John David's death would make an end to things.

Scott Ely

CHAPTER NINETEEN

It was easy to find John David. The rescue squad just followed the wire. Pick Dobine came to tell Chalmers about it.

"I was there," Pick said. "Wasn't hardly a mark on him. Not even from the wire. Turtles been charmed. Looked like he'd just woke up from a good night's sleep."

Chalmers wondered about that. He'd seen the wire loop itself around John David's neck.

Pick turned to look at Livia. She was working with a cypress log a short distance away, but because the sound the chain saw was making there was no chance she could hear what they were saying. Chalmers couldn't be certain yet exactly what she was making. It didn't look like it was going to have teeth. The lines were more like those of a canoe.

"Folks are saying that girl did it," Pick said. "I been telling 'em they're wrong." He jerked his head toward Livia.

"Did what?" Chalmers asked.

"I done told you what they say she did."

"Tell me again."

"No turtles. Come out of the river with skin as smooth as a baby's."

"Cold water."

"Brother Sprott says it's that girl."

Livia hadn't noticed they were watching her. All her concentration was on the wood under her chisel. She'd told Chalmers that she intended to add nothing to the log, only to cut the wood away until whatever was inside emerged.

"You were there?" Chalmers asked.

"Standing on the bank watching," Pick said.

"You mean you didn't help?"

Pick laughed.

"I ain't touching no drowned man," he said. "Especially one who looks like he's getting ready to wake up. Maybe grab me and drag me right down to Hell with him."

"I've got work to do," Chalmers said.

"You ain't ill with me? I'm just telling you what folks has been saying."

"Thanks."

Chalmers was going to be glad when John David was finally buried. The funeral was the next day at the Nectar Bridge Church. Livia had insisted he take her to the burial.

Livia drove them to the funeral in her van. He'd tried to persuade her to leave Ivan and Phoebe behind, but she'd insisted. She was afraid someone would come out to Plumb's Bluff and steal or destroy them. He imagined people looking through the windows at them. The statues would simply fuel more rumors about Livia.

People at the church were polite, but everyone except for Grandmother Rosa and Rudy stayed away from them. Even Edward kept his distance.

"Daddy be mad I'm even talking to you," Edward said. "They're saying all sorts of things about that woman. Worse than before."

Chalmers simply wanted to get the funeral over with and take Livia back to Plumb's Bluff.

Grandmother Rosa insisted they sit with her.

"We'll sit in the back," Chalmers said.

"I've spoken with Macon," Rosa said. "There'll be none of his foolishness."

Chalmers remembered the Brother Sprott he'd met that night on the banks of the river. He didn't see how Grandmother Rosa could reason with him.

"Once Macon gets going there ain't much way he can control what comes out of his mouth," Rudy said.

"I want you with me," Rosa said. "Livia too. For once this family is going to be together instead of apart."

"You come be with your grandmother," Rudy said.

Chalmers gave up and said he would.

They all sat together on the bench. Rudy was next to the aisle, one of his legs sprawled out in it, and Livia between Chalmers and Grandmother Rosa. The service began.

John David was laid out in his seersucker suit in a casket surrounded with roses. Any damage the barbs had done to his neck had been concealed by the undertaker. Grandmother Rosa had him dressed in his climbing harness.

"He had it on every day of his life," she said. "He'd want it that way."

Various members of the congregation stood up one by one and talked about John David. Then Grandmother Rosa got up.

"I was greedy," she said. "John David did what was buried down deep inside me. What's in all of us. I killed my son. I killed John David."

"No," Rudy moaned. "No, Rosa."

"John David saw the darkness inside me," she said. "He didn't understand. It wasn't his fault."

She began to cry. Rudy got up and put his arms around her, and then other members of the congregation followed. A group of women surrounded her and laid their hands gently on her.

"The Lord will forgive you," Brother Sprott said.

Brother Sprott's voice was calm and even. Chalmers regarded him suspiciously.

Then people began shouting "Praise the Lord!" Some came up and hugged her. Grandmother Rosa's grief was submerged beneath the enthusiasm of the congregation. She stood there by the casket, surrounded by her friends.

Rudy helped her back to the bench. Brother Sprott took over the service.

"I preached against that woman," Brother Sprott said.

He pointed his finger at Livia. Then he turned and walked over to the casket. He looked down at John David.

"I was wrong," Brother Sprott said. "That woman ain't important. I, like Sister Plumb, am full up with darkness."

He paused and looked out over the congregation. Chalmers turned to see what Brother Sprott was staring at. The rest of the people did also. But there was nothing, only the rectangle of light which marked the open door and the tops of the cars and trucks in the parking lot. The church was perfectly quiet. Everyone waited for his next words.

"You all seen this man," he said. "Who closed the mouths

of the turtles? Who brought him out of the river as fresh as a new born babe?"

Chalmers felt hemmed in. He wished he and Livia were sitting next to the door so there'd be an easy way out if Brother Sprott stirred up the crowd against her.

"Who?" Brother Sprott asked.

The crowd was silent.

"Who?" he asked.

"The devil!" a woman shouted. "Through that girl!"

"No!" Brother Sprott shouted. "No! It was the Lord that closed the turtle's mouths. It was the Lord that kept the wire from piercing his flesh. It was the Lord that brought that man out of the river. It was the Lord who made John David Weathers' skin as soft as a precious little child's. Praise the Lord!"

There were a few scattered calls of "Praise the Lord!"

"The Lord can defeat Death," Brother Sprott said. "John David is a sign to all of us. The Lord brought him shining out of that river. Let's all give the Lord a hand."

The congregation was silent for a moment.

"Come on, say hallelujah. Give the Lord a hand. Wasn't for the Lord this casket would be closed. Come on!"

"Hallelujah!" a man yelled.

His cry was taken up by others and they applauded.

"That's right," Brother Sprott yelled. "Give the Lord a hand. HE deserves it. HE saved John David from the turtles. HE brought him perfect out of the river. HE can save what is corruptible. HE can bring your souls shining out of death like a bar of gold out of the river. Spanish gold it could be. Still shining."

DeSoto had passed close to Susan Moore. Tales of lost gold and jewels still persisted.

Brother Sprott looked directly at Livia.

"It don't matter if the Devil has laid his hand on her!" he shouted. "The Lord will make her shine!"

Grandmother Rosa put her hand on Chalmers' arm.

"You carry her out of here," she said. "Wait at the graveyard."

Chalmers took Livia's hand and pulled her to her feet. Rudy got up to let them pass.

"You're welcome to stay," Brother Sprott said. "Stay and be cleansed by the Lord. Ain't nothing He can't do."

Chalmers turned and looked at the congregation.

"We're staying at the river," Chalmers said. "Nobody's gonna run us off. Yawl hear. Nobody."

The congregation was silent. People looked down at their feet, their heads bowed as if they were praying.

"Chalmers, you better get that hate out of your heart," Brother Sprott said. "The Lord will wash you clean. You ask Him."

"Go," Grandmother Rosa said.

Chalmers took Livia by the hand and led her down the aisle. It was as if she were his bride, but instead of smiles they were met with impassive, solemn faces. Some of the people, he could plainly see, were afraid. Brother Sprott was still talking about the power of the Lord over evil.

At the graveyard Livia wandered among the tombstones. A freshly dug grave was waiting for John David.

"I do nothing," Livia said.

"I know," Chalmers said.

"Let us leave this place."

"We're staying. Nobody's gonna run me off."

Chalmers considered his promise to his father. John David could have been buried in the grove of pines. But this was John David's church. It was his right to be buried here.

"Why do they think I am of the devil?" Livia asked.

"They're afraid," he said.

Through the open door they could hear Brother Sprott's voice but were too far away to understand what he was saying.

"This is a bad place to live," she said.

She wandered off among the tombstones. They were coming out of the church, following John David's coffin. The procession came up the slight rise to the cemetery. The pallbearers were winded from the walk.

Chalmers took Livia's hand and drew her close to the grave. The pallbearers looked nervous. The rest of the congregation came up to the grave. Brother Sprott had to urge them to come close.

They put the casket down on the edge of the grave. Brother Sprott spoke the words over it, and they lowered it into the ground. Everyone drifted away, leaving Chalmers and Livia along with Grandmother Rosa and Rudy.

"Least he's not in the river," Rudy said.

"He never heard Brother Sprott preach but once," Chalmers said. "Being dead is the best way to be when he's preaching."

Rudy laughed. Livia didn't understand the joke. Grandmother Rosa was crying.

"I'm sorry, Chalmers," Grandmother Rosa said. "I'm sorry for all of it."

"It's over now," Chalmers said. "They'll leave us alone."

"You come stay at Susan Moore tonight," Rudy said.

"Yes," Grandmother Rosa said.

Chalmers shook his head.

"We're going back to Daddy's trailer," he said.

The deacons were waiting by the door of the church with their shovels.

"Macon won't be preaching against Livia any more," Grandmother Rosa said.

"He don't have to," Chalmers said. "He's already done enough. Anything happens and I'm holding him responsible."

Grandmother Rosa gave Chalmers a sad look.

"Will it never end?" she asked.

"When he leaves us alone," Chalmers said.

"You could come back to the church," Rudy said.

"No," Chalmers said.

"It wouldn't do," Grandmother Rosa said. "Macon is a stubborn man."

"He's a man who wants to see folks dead," Chalmers said.

Chalmers thought again of his interview with Brother Sprott on the riverbank.

"It's over," Grandmother Rosa said. "Thank the Lord you didn't shoot anybody, Chalmers."

"John David can see to the end of the earth," Livia said. "He is the emperor of trees. He can see to Mobile."

They all laughed.

"If there're trees where he is, he's climbing," Rudy said.

Chalmers kissed his grandmother on the cheek. He shook Rudy's hand. He looked one more time at the unfilled grave. The pile of earth was red and lumpy. Chalmers imagined the sound the shovels would make in it, the clods ringing on the blades. He put his arm around Livia, and they walked together to the van.

CHAPTER TWENTY

Chalmers came home late one Sunday night from running a river in Tennessee. Livia had gone to the opening of an exhibit of her work in Birmingham. She'd promised to come home the next day. He didn't want her at Plumb's Bluff alone. He'd bought a used truck, because even the engine he'd salvaged from the flood had turned out to be beyond repair.

Livia had almost finished work on the cypress log. It had emerged as an abstract thing, but its lines were smooth and curved instead of the acute angles and hard surfaces of the toothed figures. As he came down the road to the trailer, he heard a heavy sound he couldn't identify.

He drove around a curve and saw the light reflecting off the trees tops. He smelled the sharp scent of burning epoxy. There was an explosion. He drove into the yard. Silhouetted against the burning shop was Livia, her hand raised to her face to shield herself from the heat. In the other hand she held a hose.

"Livia!" he yelled.

She motioned for him to come help fight the fire. Now there was smoke coming from the trailer. She moved closer, crouching against the heat.

He ran across the thirty yards that separated them. She thought he was coming to help with the hose, and she handed it to him. He let it drop to the ground. The heat was intense. Sparks from the fire had burned holes in her t-shirt.

"Run!" he said fiercely. "Run!"

She hesitated, but he pulled her away. There was no time to explain about the drums of acetone, the highly explosive solvent for polyester. When the fire reached it, there would be a large, violent explosion.

He pulled her across the yard. She stumbled and fell. He jerked her to her feet. They ran. A drum went up just as they reached the picnic table. He pulled her to the ground, and together they scrambled over the lip of the bluff. A tongue of flame rose high into the sky, green pine needles crackling as the fire ignited them. The trailer was burning now.

"I hear them," Livia said.

"Brother Sprott?" Chalmers asked.

"I do not know."

Brother Sprott may not have been there himself, but he was responsible.

"We must leave this place," Livia said.

"No," Chalmers said.

"Then we will stay until they kill us?"

"They won't kill us."

"You will kill them? "

And Chalmers realized she was right. He couldn't see an end to it. Brother Sprott had gone too far.

"They will burn until we die," Livia said.

"Where do you want to go?" Chalmers asked.

"Mobile."

"How will I train in Mobile?" he asked.

"Only for a little time. Then we will go to a river or the mountains."

"How will we live?"

"My sculpture. It sells good."

Chalmers tried to imagine living somewhere besides Blount County. He thought of his father's grave up in the grove of pines.

"You will win next month," she said.

Chalmers sat with his back against the lip of the bluff and listened to the fire burn. The air was filled with the stink of burning chemicals. Off in the distance he heard the sirens from the volunteer fire company. Mr. Graves, who lived in a house near the bridge, had probably seen the flames and called them.

"Wouldn't be surprised if those damn firemen set it," Chalmers said.

Livia didn't reply. She was on her feet, watching the fire burn, the light reflecting off her face.

"You will forget all of this," she said.

Chalmers laughed.

"I can't," he said. "This is my home."

"Romania was my home," Livia said. "Do you want to be burned?"

"They're trying to run us off," Chalmers said. "Not kill us."

Another explosion went off and flames and sparks shot up into the treetops. The heat washed over them. Livia crouched beside him, her hands over her head. A rain of debris fell on them.

"They will kill us," Livia said.

Chalmers imagined living in Mobile with Livia. He pictured them driving up to Tennessee or North Carolina with the canoes on the van.

"I won't have a way to live," Chalmers said. "There's no blasting to be done around Mobile."

"Win the race," Livia said. "I will sell my sculptures."

"I can't count on winning."

"Then sell the land."

He shook his head.

He doubted if she could ever be made to understand what selling would mean. The promises he had to honor that stretched across three generations.

"Sell it," she said.

"You don't understand," he said.

"I understand. But you must forget."

"I am not so sure."

"Forget."

She reached out and put her hand on his cheek. He took her in his arms. She smelled of smoke.

"I want us to live," she said.

"We're going live," he said.

The firemen were coming along the road to the trailer now. Chalmers and Livia climbed back over the lip of the bluff and watched them spray water on the dying fire. The scent of chemicals and burned wood hung in the air.

As he watched them work, Chalmers noticed the firemen acted as if he and Livia were not there. He and Livia sat on the picnic table, their arms around each other. Then the fire was out, the charred wreckage of the shop and trailer illuminated by the lights from the firemen's trucks.

Earl Wright, the fire chief, walked over to the picnic table.

"Wasn't much we could do, Chalmers," Earl said.

Earl was old enough to be Chalmers' father. He owned the store at the crossroads. Chalmers didn't reply. Chalmers heard and felt Livia's breathing quicken.

"Could be arson," Earl said. "But you got all them chemicals about. Gonna be hard to tell."

"You know what it was," Chalmers said.

"What?" Earl asked.

"You've been in church," Chalmers said.

"We come out here and risk our lives," Earl said. "You got all them chemicals in that shop. Something could've blowed up and killed us all."

"Everything blew before you came," Chalmers said.

"What're you trying to say?" Earl asked.

"That you know who did this," Chalmers said.

"I was home asleep when I got a call," Earl said. "We put out fires. We don't start them. Is that what you're saying?"

"You know who started it."

Earl sighed.

"Chalmers, you're on a false scent," Earl said. "You think it's arson then you call the sheriff."

Earl turned and walked away. The firemen loaded their equipment and left the bluff.

Chalmers took a flashlight from the truck. He and Livia walked among the still smoking remains of the trailer and shop. Nothing was left of the shop except for Livia's unfinished marble plug.

"A stone boat," Livia said.

They both laughed.

Chalmer's spare boats had been destroyed, but he'd make a mold from the one of the two boats up on the racks on his truck.

"We go to Mobile, tonight?" Livia asked.

"No," Chalmers said.

"Please?"

"We'll stay at Susan Moore."

Livia wanted him to forget. Some things he thought he could, but that promise was impossible to wipe out of his mind. He'd never sell Plumb's Bluff.

"Tomorrow we go to Mobile?" Livia said.

"No," he said.

"We talk about it tomorrow."

"We can talk, but I'm not leaving. Maybe you should go to Mobile for a few days while I clean up this place."

He wanted her to stay, not leave, but he was afraid for her.

"If you stay, I stay."

She kissed him.

They loaded the unfinished cypress sculpture into the van. Livia followed him to Susan Moore. His grandmother's house was dark. He rang the bell and watched it fill up with light.

Grandmother Rosa sat there stiff and motionless as if she'd been carved out of stone, while Chalmers told her about the fire. Rudy had just come home from his cows. The scent of manure was on his clothes. Rudy put one of his big hands around a coffee cup. The wrinkles and splits in his skin were filled with dirt.

"Stay as long as you want," Grandmother Rosa said.

Chalmers and Livia went to bed in John David's room. It was here that Chalmers had lain and been terrified of trains. The room still smelled of John David, that stale locker room smell of sweat from the man whose body had been constantly in motion. An article about John David's climb of the tallest tree in Blount County was taped to the wall.

He lay in bed with Livia but found it difficult to sleep.

"Sleep, Chalmers," she said.

He wrapped his arms around her and waited for sleep. Soon Livia slept and then he did. But it didn't seem as if he'd slept but a few seconds when he woke with a start. He thought he smelled smoke. He sat up in bed. Livia groaned in her sleep. The screenless window was a light rectangle against the darkness of the room. The moon rode in the branches of the big oak. Cicadas hummed in the tree. A sweet scent from a flower tree near the road drifted through the window.

He got out of bed and walked to the window. Then, thinking of John David as he did it, he stepped out of the window and onto the limb, which swayed under his weight. He looked at the chess set below. All he could make out were the dark shapes of the pieces. He reached the trunk and climbed up on the next highest limb. Carefully he made his way to the top of the tree. He'd wanted to go high but not as high as John David.

Finally he reached a place where he could see the ridge. On

the other side of it was the gorge that held the river. Off in the darkness lights were scattered here and there, but the ridge was completely dark.

For a long time he sat in the tree, looking at the ridge and listening to the calls of the night birds that were hunting insects high above the security light near the road. The scent of the flower tree rose up to him. A breeze came up, and the tree swayed slightly. The scent of the flower tree was diffused, but he could still smell it if he concentrated.

Then the breeze stopped and everything was still again. The insects hummed madly from the trees across the road. He remained in his perch until that sweet scent of the flower tree rose up to him again, now so sweet that it was almost cloying. He looked off in the direction of the river and the Nectar Bridge church. The church lay empty and dark, waiting for Brother Sprott to fill it with hate.

As he descended, the flower-tree scent became weaker. He entered the room and returned to bed, taking Livia, who murmured in her sleep, in his arms. But he found it difficult to sleep. He got up and dressed. With his running shoes in his hands, he walked barefoot out of the room and down the stairs and out of the house. He sat on the front steps and put on his shoes.

From Livia's van he took a pair of bolt cutters. He got a backpack and the mountain bike from his truck. Then he went off down the road. No one was out. It was two in the morning. He pumped the bike hard and rode the five miles to the strip mine where he cut the lock to the gate.

The bike's tires hissed in the soft dust as he rode through the deserted mine. He cut the padlock to the explosives shack and filled the backpack with dynamite and a coil of detonation cord. He went to Rudy's trailer and pried the door open. He took a box of blasting caps.

Then he rode back along the deserted roads to the Nectar Bridge Church. Only once did he meet a car. He pulled the bike off the road and into a clump of pines and waited for it to pass. He crossed the Nectar Bridge and went up the hill towards the church.

Chalmers found the door of the church open. He took the bike inside and sat on his family's bench and considered how best to blow the church. No one would get hurt. For himself it would make an end to things, a fair exchange for the fire at Plumb's

Bluff.

The church was cinder block and rafters, the roof metal. If they'd used steel in its construction, he'd have needed plastic explosive to cut the rafters and wall joists at the proper places. This was going to be easy.

He simply taped clusters of five sticks of dynamite into the corners of the room and the center of the walls, places where the rafters rested on the top of the concrete blocks. He stood on a stepladder he found in a closet to do it. He wished he could drill holes into the blocks and drop in the sticks, but he imagined that what he was doing was enough to blow out the walls and drop the roof down into the church.

He worked steadily. By the time he finished, it was four o'clock, leaving him just enough time to ride home in the cover of darkness. He ran the wires out the front door and hooked them up to the blasting machine behind the big tree John David had climbed.

By habit he wanted to check the circuit, but he couldn't see to do it. He told himself it didn't matter. The woods were quiet. The moon had set. Somewhere way off on the river he heard dogs running, their baying so faint the sound of it came and went. It was probably Dobines running their dogs after a coon. He looked at the church, white and silent in the darkness. He put his finger on the blasting button.

Chalmers thought of the people filing into the church, his neighbors. It was Brother Sprott who had made them afraid. He recalled Livia's injunction to forget.

Then Brother Sprott walked into Chalmer's field of vision. The preacher strode across the gravel, walking right over the wires. He walked around the side of the church. Chalmers wondered if someone had seen him go inside the church. Perhaps Brother Sprott was accustomed to check the church once or twice each night. In a few minutes he appeared again. Chalmers hoped he wouldn't go inside. He'd be sure to see the det cord.

Brother Sprott walked across the gravel. When he reached the road, Chalmers pressed the button. A huge flash illuminated the night, and the whine of the insects was silenced by the roar of the explosion.

Pieces of the church fell down through the trees, making a sound like a heavy rain against the leaves. Chalmers smelled the stink of the explosion. Brother Sprott was sprawled on the road. Chalmers heard him yelling something but couldn't understand the words. Then he heard Brother Sprott's feet on the gravel. He was running for his trailer.

Chalmers stood up and looked at the church. The roof had dropped down on top of the benches. For some reason one wall had held. A cloud of smoke hung over the ruined church like an early morning fog that had drifted up from the river.

The nearest house, besides Brother Sprott's trailer—where the preacher had lived alone since his wife had died—was five miles away. The explosion must have shattered the windows in the trailer.

The congregation would rebuild it. He'd rebuild the shop and put a new trailer at Plumb's Bluff.

Chalmers picked up the blasting machine and popped the wires off it. He put the machine in the now empty backpack and went off down the road. The road sloped downward toward the river, and the bike's tires kept losing purchase on the gravel. He stopped on the bridge. He looked down at the dark water and thought of Livia standing there that day between Ivan and Phoebe. He carefully wiped the blasting machine clean with his shirt. Then he tossed it into the river where in the darkness it made a splash that seemed too large for its size.

Chalmers rode hard for Susan Moore, mostly across fields and through the woods so he wouldn't be seen by those awakened by the explosion. He slipped into the dark house.

Livia was asleep. He lay down beside her. She rolled over. He was shaking as he lay there, holding desperately to Livia and taking slow even breaths. She didn't wake. The sweat gradually dried on his body, its scent adding to that of John David's.

At the moment he'd pressed the button on the blasting machine, he'd felt free and light. But now he felt as if he were in a canoe on an unfamiliar river on a moonless night with a broken paddle in his hands and a huge standing wave was looming before him. For the first time it occurred to him that all his efforts to conceal the fact that he had destroyed the church wouldn't amount to much. He'd be the first person the sheriff would come looking for. He might lie and force them to try him, or he might admit it and do his time. He wondered if Livia would be there for him when he finished his sentence. She could wait in Mobile.

Scott Ely

The sound of the baying hounds drifted through the open window. He listened to them for a long time, waiting for the light. But the light never came. Time seemed to have stopped. He wrapped his arms around Livia and little by little the heavy feeling in his body drained away. He wanted to sleep long and deep. Waking was going to be hard.

Scott Ely was born in Atlanta, GA, and he moved to Jackson, MS when he was eight. He served in Vietnam (somewhere in the highlands near Pleiku). He graduated with an MFA from the University of Arkansas, Fayetteville. He taught fiction writing at Winthrop University in South Carolina. His previous book publications include STARLIGHT (Weidenfeld & Nicolson); PITBULL (Weidenfeld & Nicolson, Penguin); OVERGROWN WITH LOVE (University of Arkansas Press); THE ANGEL OF THE GARDEN (University of Missouri Press); PULPWOOD (Livingston Press); and A SONG FOR ALICE LOOM (Livingston Press). His work has been translated in Italy, Germany, Israel, Poland, and Japan. There were also UK editions of several novels published. Scott died in November, before he could see this novel's publication.